The Most Distant Way

The Most Distant Way

Ewan Gault

Holland House

www.hhousebooks.com

Hardback ISBN	978-1-909374-48-5
Paperback ISBN	978-1-909374-49-2
Kindle ISBN	978-1-909374-50-8
Epub	978-1-909374-51-5

Cover design by Ken Dawson.

Published in the USA and UK

Holland House Books
Holland House
47 Greenham Road
Newbury
Berkshire
RG14 7HY

United Kingdom

www.hhousebooks.com

For all those who run the long and lonely roads

PERTH & KINROSS COUNCIL	
05721112	
Bertrams	27/12/2013
	£7.99
AKB	

Acknowledgements

For their advice, encouragement, good humour and patience, I would like to thank Lauren Nicoll, John Douglas Millar, Francesca Campanozzi, Robert Barnes, Dougal Squires, Laura Yuile, Ed Wilkinson and Laura Bulloch, and my editor Robert Peett. I am particularly grateful to my parents for all their support over the years. I would lastly like to thank all the friends I have made when travelling, teaching and running when far away from home.

The most distant way in the world
is not the way from birth to the end

Rabindranath Tagore

Chapter One

At the end of a nameless road, after passing schoolgirls playing by sewage-sludged streams, their brilliant white socks and gleaming smiles implausible amongst the rust and the rot, near the pavement strewn with ragged rows of men with nothing to do but stare at the passing westerners, we were ambushed by a gang of street children.

Their leader was a boy of about eight who smiled with the innocence of someone who has never seen a camera before. He wore a Dundee United away strip from the early nineties, with the name Malpas on the back.

"You! How are you?" he chanted in my face.

Kirsten got off her bike, her nostrils flaring in the thin air; paw prints of sweat padding out from the underarms of her T-shirt.

"You have been lost," Malpas exclaimed.

"How are you?" Kirsten asked.

"Very ok. And you?"

"Somehow ok."

"The way these people speak English is bad enough," I told her, "you shouldn't encourage them."

Malpas clicked his fingers and the other children surrounded us placing their free hands on the seat, handlebar and frame of my bike. Kirsten let go of her bike, laughing and patting the children's sheared heads. Shuffling in front of us, Malpas lifted one hand, cupped plaintively in my direction, posing like a poster child for charity. I avoided his unblinking stare, not wanting to see the yolk yellow sclera or the bottle of honey hued glue that he, like every other kid, clutched jealously to his side.

Clearly some Scottish charity had been doing good work here for other members of the gang were sporting the worst Technicolor football strips of the previous decade, including a lilac Rangers monstrosity, a moss-patched Celtic top and a white Scotland strip with a splash of purple and jagged red lines across the front.

Malpas stopped backtracking and the hands helping my bike clamped it in place. "Mzungo, some shillings please."

I shook my head and pulled out the linings of my pockets.

"Look, no money," I said.

A toddler with a wizened face started stroking my arm; the red hairs held an endless fascination for all Kenyan children, but now he was eyeing my watches. Remembering a taxi driver telling me about a tourist having her wrist macheted by some kids wanting to steal her Rolex, I wrenched my arm away.

"Why you wear two watches?" Malpas asked.

I looked to Kirsten for help, but she was delving into her ugly hemp satchel. She started handing out small coins to the boys around her even though I'd explained it would only encourage them to make a profession of begging.

Someone tugged at my rucksack's zip. Spinning round, I saw a couple of boys dancing away, their faces sticky with glue and glee. Prickling with sweat and the blush of a ridiculous rage, I pulled the bike from the others.

The boys let go and I stumbled back.

"Thank you," I said, but they weren't listening. A tour bus, shiny and strange as a UFO, had appeared on the road. It stopped and a group of Japanese tourists clad in safari outfits, with bulging bum bags and fat black cameras, gathered on the street. The street boys licked their lips.

"Do you know them?" Malpas asked.

"No," I replied. "They're Japanese, why would I know them?"

"Japanese." He chewed apprehensively on the word so that the others laughed. He nodded but I could see he wasn't convinced.

A tour guide waving a triangular white flag led the tourists up the street. One took a picture of the tour bus then spun around looking for something else worth capturing. Another pointed out the minarets of an Oil State funded mosque that sat on the edge of the city like a wedding cake on a rubbish heap. I felt like shouting, "No lions here!" A younger floppy-haired man lifted a Canon fitted with a massive zoom lens and took a photo of The Wonder Café. I thought of my own cheap camera and how afraid I was to point it anywhere in case people took offence. The floppy-haired tourist aimed at a group of old men eating sweetcorn. He managed to take the photo before they spoilt it by looking at the camera and smiling. The old men nudged each other and laughed as the photographer rejoined his group. They seemed happy. It was, after all, a big camera.

The boys ghosted across the street, splitting into groups of twos and threes. As inconspicuous as their day-glo football strips allowed them to be, they approached the herd. The Japanese looked confused, twitching at hidden wallets and money belts. Watching the gang's stealth and silence I realised that they were only ever playing with me.

I caught up with Kirsten and we joined the sweaty, agitated throng surrounding the bus station's office. People sat on suitcases, their heads resting on crossed arms as if they'd been waiting for days. Others paced the floor, shouting threats and pleas at the officials over the sound of crying babies. A man with an important-looking hat sat slumped behind a desk. Occasionally he would attempt to swat a fly before looking with extreme irritation at his fingers to see if he had killed it. At no point did he look at the ruck of dusty humanity trying to catch his attention. This was the role of a jockey-sized official who indiscriminately selected individuals from the crowd and bade them come and buy tickets. Any hope that foreigners would get preferential treatment was quickly dashed by the example of two Chinese men, probably road building contractors, who had become furious with the system and were berating the little man. He, however, was far more interested in the state of his cuffs. Only once did he deign to look at them and that was to say, "I'm sorry, but is that English you are speaking? I really can't understand a thing." While one Chinese man restrained the other the official assumed a bored look which barely concealed his intense satisfaction.

Realising the hopelessness of our predicament, I panicked and said, "We're going to be stuck in this hell hole. Something's gone wrong. These people are trying to escape."

"Stop exaggerating Mike, they're simply trying to get home for Christmas."

As usual, her casual pragmatism silenced me.

"Let's stand next to these Chinese men," she whispered. I couldn't see how this would work but followed her, surreptitiously sniffing myself in an effort to confirm whether it was I who smelt of orange juice past its sell-by date. Within minutes we were called forward. One of the Chinese men groaned and started shouting what were undoubtedly obscenities. The little official pulled out seats for us, nodding and smiling all the time. We sat at a table behind which worked a girl with milky, mud puddle skin and dark freckles. She spoke to us in a hushed voice that seemed to show deference to the man in the important hat.

I let Kirsten deal with the booking. She had a way of making herself understood in these situations. "Two tickets for Nairobi to leave on Monday the 17th and two day tickets from Nairobi to Mombasa, leaving on the 18th," she said, pointing out the dates on a calendar.

"By the way, why do you not make the return?" the important-hatted man asked.

"Because we're going home."

"Good." He nodded, picking up a mango and noisily slurping on it. The girl at the desk sat very still, pen poised, eyes on the calendar. "Documents," said the man.

"Sorry?"

"Your papers, you surely have your papers?"

"I'm sorry but we don't have them with us at the moment." I said.

"Oh?" He flopped back in his chair, a look of immense satisfaction spreading across his face. "This does disturb me." On one wall, as to be expected, was an official framed photo of the President and on the other a portrait of a young and quite dapper Saddam Hussein. The man with the important hat sat between them.

"Our passports are in the orphanage of Mr K. We are his guests," Kirsten said, which was ostensibly true, even though we had only seen the legendary former athlete twice. "We are helping at his orphanage and also training with some local runners at the high altitude centre."

I had forgotten how posh Kirsten could sound when talking to authority. The name of one of the city's most famous sons, a man who had a street, school and running camp named after him had a predictable effect. The official removed his important hat and wiped his shiny scalp with a handkerchief.

"I see," he said. "You are surely Americans?"

"No, British," Kirsten corrected him.

"Scottish," I said.

"You Scottish?" The man addressed me affectionately. "You know what it is like to be oppressed, I have seen your film, Braveheart. This young man," he flapped a hand in Kirsten's direction, "understands nothing. He cannot know how many comforts the story of your Mel Gibson is giving to the afflicted peoples."

"No," I agreed. "*She* doesn't."

The man rattled off some Kiswahili to the girl, who immediately started writing out our tickets.

"I have told her to give you the specialist seats in front of the bus. We hope you are enjoying them."

As we struggled back to our bikes, I let out a little whoop of excitement.

Kirsten winced. "What was that?"

She scratched a weeping wound on her thigh from where a mosquito had bitten her. Her hands looked clean enough but her fingernails would be harbouring colonies of bacteria. I thought about telling her but instead said, "Joy at getting out of this place alive."

Shaking her head, she said, "Can we go to the supermarket? I want to buy some biscuits."

"Biscuits?"

"Yeah, you can give a packet to the men you're building the roof with and I'll give some to the women in the orphanage."

Kirsten smiled, sincere as a talk show host. Spending all this time with her had made me long to see her mask slip. She gave the impression of always being good without ever being kind. I believed she hated me, and this idea made me confused, excited and at times a little despondent. "That's a great idea," I said.

We had to pass the University, where students were plastering posters of the presidential candidates over a billboard with the winning slogan, GET A DEGREE NOT HIV. Hundreds of young men sat around the sign watching us.

Kirsten stared straight ahead. She was the same height as me and walked so fast that I had to skip an extra step every so often to keep up with her. As I walked by her side trying to start a conversation I was never sure if I looked like a child trying to catch an adult's attention or just another predatory male.

At the market, women tried to sell us bead necklaces, carved candle stick holders and water carriers made out of animal hides.

"These are sick," Kirsten said, picking up some tortured looking wooden masks.

We were going home in a week and I still hadn't bought Christmas presents, so I stopped to look at some pottery. A chubby woman with shiny cheeks and a dress colourful as a carnival asked, "Can you promote me? 200 shillings, number one top price." She waded towards us, every jiggle looking like the start of a dance. "You make your wife so happy with this." Kirsten batted her eyelids, and pouted like a spoilt child.

"She's not actually my wife." The two women laughed conspiratorially, and I pulled my money out.

The vases would probably have cost 20 times as much in the type of ethnic shop in Britain that people like Kirsten frequent. Here, though, I felt harassed, suspicious that the vendor, Kirsten and the crowd, touching my arms and tugging on my T-shirt with their grubby hands, were conspiring in some embarrassing fraud. I put on one of my surgical gloves and handed the fat woman some dirty notes, certain that I was doing her a great favour.

The supermarket gave an impression of exclusivity, protected as it was by two armed guards and brutally efficient air conditioning. I had tried living like a Kenyan athlete for the last three months but when you start breaking into the cough syrup and laxative chocolates for a night time sugar fix you know that something's got to give. Grabbing a basket, I strode along the tiled floor, rejoicing in the cleanliness and silence of the place. I had been having the sort of food fantasies one normally associates with pregnant women. This time it was condensed milk and Pop Tarts. I was convinced that these and these alone could give me the energy needed to get through this evening's interval sessions.

When we met at the checkout I felt the need to explain. "I'd never eat this stuff at home, but I can't resist. I'm starving—all this packaging and advertising. The Kenyan runners are lucky really that they don't have this temptation."

"I'm sure they'd see things a little differently," Kirsten replied, holding the packets of biscuits out to one side in the way posh ladies hold doggy bags. Her hair, which inexplicably she had been shaving skinhead-short for the past two years, had grown and been bleached blonde by the sunlight during our three months in Kenya. With her pixie nose and concave cheeks she looked like one of those androgynous models who appear in adverts for French perfume.

We split the cost of the counterfeit biscuits: party rings, Rich Teas and digestives in packaging that looked almost like the real thing. The Pop Tarts, as with most Western branded products, were much more expensive, but that wasn't important to me.

"Do you know they're planning a going-away party for us?" Kirsten said as we put the shopping in my back pack.

"I had no idea."

"I heard them talking in the kitchen. Agnes is saving sugar to make a cake. She's never made a cake before."

"That sounds promising."

"They want us to do some kind of performance, a dance I think."

As we cycled towards the market I noticed that the street was emptying. The stallholders were folding up the cardboard boxes that had doubled as tables, and making the cotton sheets on which their wares had been displayed into makeshift bags.

Suddenly, a few hundred men came roaring round the corner, bolting bug-eyed and wild towards us. I turned my bike to pedal away, but Kirsten was going nowhere.

"Look," she said, and sure enough the men had slowed and were dabbing puckered cuts on their heads and bunching back together. Many were waving dusty palm branches the way people did when there was a traffic accident, a cow running amok or a visiting dignitary passing through.

"Let's get out of here," I hissed. "It's some kind of demonstration."

"Don't be pathetic, Mike. This could be interesting."

The last few stallholders were making their escape, and even the laziest of the onlookers were getting to their feet and edging away. Keeping pace with them seemed the best option but Kirsten was intent on getting us in trouble.

"Following a man who's running away isn't always a good idea," she said.

This was debatable, but I didn't want her to think me a

coward. "What's with all the orange T-shirts?"

"It shows their affiliation with Odaiga."

This meant nothing to me so I said, "I think you're right."

We were far enough from the crowd that we could see over their heads. Around the corner strode a police officer, fat and calmly officious in his dark green shirt and black beret, armed with only a bamboo stick and whistle. He swiped at the legs of the protesters, who withdrew from him like hyenas before a lion. The officer was followed by five more policemen all holding rifles pointed to the heavens. The crowd screeched and, emboldened by their shared indignation, shuffled forward. It was only then that I realised Kirsten had rested her camera on the bike's handlebars and was filming the whole thing.

"It's against the law to film the police," I said. "Stop it. I'm serious. They've got guns."

On cue, a shot cracked through the muggy afternoon. Wailing, the crowd split in all directions. I ducked behind my bike as if they were aiming at me; as if the bike offered protection.

"He only shot in the air. It sounded like a blank anyway." Kirsten announced, as if she knew what blanks sounded like. A barrage of shots rang out and suddenly the protesters were rushing around us, but not with that graceful tall stride we'd seen when training with local athletes. These people ran the way people on newsreels around the world do: dodging imagined bullets, crouching low to the ground, trying to make themselves as small a target as possible.

I abandoned my bike and chased after them, delighted to be putting as much distance between myself and whatever was happening behind. Around me people shrieked, in terror and joy.

Protesters hugged and struggled with each other, as if to confirm that they were intact and could stand and face the police again. A couple more shots rang out but the police were following another group of demonstrators who had escaped in a different direction. Squinting through the russet dust kicked up by the retreating feet, I saw Kirsten crouched behind her bike, camera still in hand. A man howled and pointed at what looked like our gang of street children as they dragged one of their day-glo'd number from the road. I was caught up in the gathering fury as the protesters turned and charged after the police. Men pulled and dragged me down the road and I was thrust rudely in Kirsten's direction.

"What the fuck are you doing? We have to get out of here!" I snatched her camera, picked up my bike and began pedalling frantically, with her in hot pursuit. We raced through a part of the town that looked like it had been hit by a hurricane. Presumably there was some sort of order to the ramshackle mess of metal, old truck tyres and sheeting but I certainly couldn't see it. Once the tidal roar of the protest ebbed away and all I could hear was a distant sound, soft as sobs, I stopped. The air in the streets was head-achingly heavy. Eyes watched us from dirty shop windows, through dark, dank doorways.

"Can I get my camera back?"

I thought about throwing it down a drainage hole.

"What was that all about? You could have got us shot."

"Camera."

I handed it to her.

"I'm stopping at the internet café. You can cycle home alone if you want."

I caught up with her on Nandi Street where life seemed to be going on as if nothing had happened. We parked our bikes next to a plastic Christmas tree whose fairy lights flashed inconsequentially in the sun.

On the walls of the internet café a Ferrari calendar from the year before last, an aerial photo of Mecca, two traditional Chinese ink paintings and a Wonderbra advert rudely ripped from a magazine marked the tide line of international culture. People stared at screens for news from distant lands like immigrants in past times hanging out in harbours, waiting for gossip from home. Rules and regulations, most of which were capitalised and highlighted in luminous green, were posted on bare patches of wall. The only thing that made it feel different from any inner-city internet cafe in Britain was the guard with the Kalashnikov at the door.

At the back of the café a stand up Coca Cola sponsored refrigerator hummed softly. Inside were rows of cans, cold and clean. "Want one?" I asked Kirsten who answered *no* by wrinkling her nose. There were seven computers of a vintage only seen in skips or lofts in Britain. I sat next to three generations of an Indian family who were picnicking around their keyboard whilst weeping and wailing at the webcam.

Waiting for my computer to log on, I rolled the cold can back and forth across my forehead before cracking the ring pull open. Kirsten meanwhile was watching the afternoon's protest silently descend into chaos on the small screen of her camera.

"Did you see something?"

"It's hard to know on this. Man that was brutal, just brutal." She chewed her lower lip. I wasn't sure if she was talking about me running away or the protest. "That's it," she said, pulling a usb cable from her bag.

"What are you doing with that?"

"I'm going to email the film to some news channels and newspapers. There's nothing on their sites about what's going on out here."

My face must have shown what I thought of this idea. I asked, "Can I see it then?"

"What?"

"Whatever you filmed that made your eyes water."

"That's not a good idea, it's not something that would . . . interest you."

To show how uninterested I was, I looked up racing results from home.

"Who do you think won the District cross-countries?" Kirsten drummed the table, waiting for the film to upload. "Ah, one of the Wilson twins. You'll beat them easily enough after all the training out here."

"That's what everyone will think."

"Your brother won the 1500m at some big meeting in the States."

"Yeah, the N.C.A.A indoors." She pronounced it like some razzmatazz sports presenter. "It was all my dad wrote about last week."

"That's pretty cool though. That he's doing so well out there I mean."

"Shit. This isn't working."

"What?"

"This computer hasn't got a program that'll allow me to upload the film. Can I try yours?"

"It's closing time and besides, whatever you've got on that camera could cause us and the people on it a lot of trouble."

"For fuck's sake Mike, grow a pair."

"I don't know what you saw that you think is so important but it's gone, past. Sending that film isn't going to help anyone."

"So we just pretend it didn't happen?"

"The world doesn't have to pretend. It isn't interested. End of. The reason you can't find any reports in British newspapers about the election or whatever's going on out here is that no one wants to know."

"This could change that," she said, shaking the camera at me, tendons on her neck quivering, her eyes filling with tears. A crazy girl in hand-me-down clothes, Celtic tattoos, African jewellery and red plastic clogs. Somehow startling beautiful, even if she was in a tribe totally of her own.

"We really don't have time. Maybe tomorrow." I went to the counter and paid for our session.

"Welcome again." The man smiled as he handed back my change. I put the notes into a resealable sandwich bag so they wouldn't touch my skin and hid the package inside my sock. After handling the money I cleaned my hands with antiseptic wipes.

As we collected our bikes, I noticed crumbling cathedrals of cumulus nimbus in the direction of Lake Victoria. Soon they would collapse across the whole sky and the afternoon's thunder storm would begin. We cycled past The Glorious Barbers and into our gang of street children, who were hanging about outside the Wellness Butcher's with its blood-speckled window and hanging hooks.

A boy who looked like he had been in a fight halted Kirsten and sullenly said, "Mother, father, sister dead, hello you, hello fine, hello 10 shillings."

Kirsten for once looked uncomfortable and I intervened, "She's already given you money."

"Mother, father, sister dead, hello you, hello fine, hello 10 shillings," the boy insisted.

"Where is your friend?" Kirsten asked. "Where is," she looked imploringly at me, "Malpas?"

"Malpas? Who he?"

"The boy . . . shit, we never even knew his name." They shuffled closer, their jaundiced eyes on me as they barged each other for position. This close, the toxic stench of their glue stained tops seared my nostrils and left my brain feeling like it was starting to melt.

Kirsten wiped her eyes. Inspired, I took a packet of biscuits from my bag and handed it to the boy. "Don't fight over these," I warned.

"10 shilling," the head boy demanded.

"If I give you money, you'll only spend it getting high. You'll go out of your minds if you keep sniffing that stuff."

"Where else should we go," the new leader snapped, waving at the open sewer behind them. "10 shilling, tomorrow."

"Ok, tomorrow," I promised, fairly certain I would never see him again.

"Me tomorrow, me tomorrow, me tomorrow," the other boys wailed, their faces desperate and doubtful, full of anger and pity for my lies. I looked at their day-glo strips, at legs so skinny their bulbous knees seemed deformed, at swollen dirty feet and calcified toenails that reminded me of dried out slivers of soap.

"Tomorrow," I repeated.

Chapter Two

Do you remember the times when thunderstorms growled and you felt childishly protected? Rain crackling crazy hard on the tin roof of a bike shed. Fine hairs on your arms bristling as the soaking earth gave up its real smells. Man, times like those gave me a mad urge to dance. Here at the back of the orphans' block I had one of those moments. I spied roses waiting to be harvested in the giant green house, bobbing their heads like spectators fighting for a view. I stepped out into the rain and curtsied.

"Shall we make a run for it?" Mike asked. "On average these afternoon storms last 27 minutes. I don't want to wait here for 27 minutes."

"Does my company horrify you that much?"

"It's not that. This place is probably full of poisonous spiders."

"I can't see any."

"You don't see them, they see you." Thunder rumbled in a great black cloud. "What are you going to do with that video?"

"Moses has a computer, maybe *he* will help me."

Mike eyed the play area, the birling pleats of rain, and the distant flashes of lightning. He seemed about to ask a question but instead pulled his T-shirt over his head like a prisoner going to court and sprinted across the yard.

I watched him disappear round the side of the building: an over grown child who weighed himself every morning, took vitamin and iron supplements with his meals, talked constantly about the diseases you can catch out here and knew the Latin names of all the animals that could bite.

Do you know how rare it was, for a white girl, to be left

alone in a country like this? How sacred those few moments were, how I cultivated and coveted my little parcels of peace?

"For you." Mike reappeared, shoving his waterproof running jacket into my hands. It smelt of old sweat, Deep Heat and Vaseline. Not bad really, *an honest smell* my father would have said.

We sprinted round the complex of buildings to the porch at the front. Three little girls I always thought of as sisters and who had names from old black and white films were tying up their skipping ropes.

I expected Mike to sneak off to his room but instead he pulled two small pink plastic containers from his pocket.

"I found these when I was packing," he explained. "My father must have put them in my suitcase to give to the children."

Solemnly, the girls watched as he stuck a spatula into one of the plastic containers, pulled it out and held it up to his lips; he blew three perfect bubbles. The sisters shrieked in delight and jumped up, trying to catch the bubbles without bursting them. Mike blew more and other children, hearing the excitement, came running out. Soon the whole porch was full of kids their bright white teeth and shining eyes.

Sylvia, the youngest sister, screamed as a bubble burst in her hands, then clapped when another swarm appeared.

"Look at the colours!" she squealed.

"It's called destructive interference," said Mike, before going on about wavelengths and light and stuff no one wanted to hear. This was typical of him. Only last week I'd caught him describing and miming the symptoms of various waterborne diseases to children as they played with little boats in a puddle. Now, sensing that he wasn't adding to the occasion he gave his bottle to an older boy called Sammy and slipped into the farmhouse. Unfortunately Sammy hadn't quite understood the procedure and promptly took a swig from the container.

Agnes, who had come from the kitchen to watch, grabbed the bottle before he could drink too much. Man, you should have seen the poor soul stick out his tongue, roll his eyes and do a little jig on the spot. Agnes slapped his legs for his troubles and pulled him into the house. His friends groaned in delight, crowding after him to see what kind of trouble he was in. Agnes confiscated the boy's bottle and tried to snatch the other one from Edith.

"These," she said, "are good for washing dishes," but in the excited melée most of the liquid was lost.

Unnoticed, the storm had stopped and the whole damp world sweating a compost stink was ready to be conquered. The children armed with skipping ropes and scabby footballs invaded the play area. Mike reappeared carrying a can of condensed milk and his Swiss Army pen knife that had enough functions to allow a man to cut down a small tree whilst plucking his eyebrows.

"You could go to the kitchen and ask for a can opener."

"Got a can opener. Besides Agnes is with the kid that drank the bubble liquid."

"Is he okay?"

"A bit disappointed that he can't blow bubbles out his nose but otherwise fine."

Eventually he opened the can without severing a finger and sipped the milk.

"Is it good?"

He deliberated for some seconds before declaring, "It's disgusting."

"Don't cut your lip."

"I can't believe I've been dreaming of this stuff for days. It's sickeningly sweet."

Before I could stop him he poured the rest of the milk onto the ground and walked into the house. Sometimes I was ashamed to be with him. While the milk soaked into the earth, I watched the children play, their flower print hand-me-down dresses and the fresh sparkle of the rain on the trees. The Christian Cow walked across the football pitch and stood chewing pensively as the boys ran around him. Sammy, who this year had the privilege of slaughtering the cow for the Christmas feast, slapped its fattening flank. I kicked some wet dirt into the puddle of condensed milk, hoping it would disappear.

Soon it was time to change for the evening run. There is nothing really to be said about that. My mind always goes dead the moment I start getting ready to train. I don't have any weird rituals to speak of. Some girls I've raced against tied and retied their laces a certain number of times; others had socks, hair bands and underwear that were worn unwashed until they become as tattered as the corner of a saint's rag hanging in an empty church.

Sometimes the lines of a poem from primary school or a pop song chorus flit across my mind and I repeat words that mean nothing to me. These are the rhythms I run to. The lines change all the time. It doesn't really matter. They are just something to cling to; a way to get through the punishing sessions.

I like doing my stretches in private. Even when racing at a big meet I would try and find some corner of a corridor in the cold concrete heart of the track's stadium. I started with the neck then on to the shoulders, hold a stretch and count elephants. I didn't notice my calf muscles burn, my right ankle crackle like a child twisting bubble wrap. I found it best not to think about my tender Achilles. Some athletes fall in love with their body when stretching, stroking themselves and marveling at their muscles. For me, looking at my thunder thighs or fat butt filled me with anger. I chewed on that anger like a ball of gum that doesn't dissolve and can't be digested or spat anywhere without somebody telling. Eventually you swallow it. When I was a kid my mum had told me swallowed chewing gum takes seven years to pass through you. Anger, I imagine, takes longer.

In the toilet I vomited a string of acrid phlegm, about enough to fill an egg cup. I wiped my mouth with the back of my hand and drank some bottled water. The girl in the mirror brushed her teeth, eyes red and watery. I was getting worse, before I used to get this nervous only before races. Now I vomited before training and even the thought of competing made me feel queasy. I rubbed my stomach; it felt better empty. I spat, cleaned it from the sink and went out to join the others.

Mike had problems with his IT band and was doing elaborate stretches on the dry floor of the porch. The Kenyans bobbed about like an audience watching a band. I never saw them doing more than the most rudimentary stretching. Did they do it in secret or did they not need to? Or did they do it in secret so they looked like they didn't need to? Did people think the same about me? Mike was lying on his back and the tips of his toes were touching the ground behind his head. He looked very much like he was trying to give himself a blow job. Perhaps that was why the Kenyans seemed uneasy.

With us this evening were two of K's children: Moses who had just returned from his first term of a sports scholarship at a Canadian University, and his younger sister, Joyce, who my parents had looked after during her five years at one of Edinburgh's best boarding schools. Joyce hated running but seemed to do it effortlessly despite her other indulgences. She smiled at me conspiratorially. Joyce thought I was the same as her and just hadn't realised it yet.

The group was completed by Sylvia and Faith, who were staying in the part of the High Altitude Centre that had just been built. They had won gold and silver medals in the summer's Junior African Championships. I liked both of them but they were shy around the rest of us. The final member was Alfred, an orphan who had grown up on the farm and now did various manual jobs about the place. His older brother, a really good runner, had defected to race for Qatar a few years ago, but no one ever mentioned him.

The two girls nodded benevolently at me. Their hair was shorn even shorter than mine and their legs were shiny and thin. Eventually Mike finished and put on his Ray Ban yellow lens sunglasses. He thought they gave the impression that he was all steely and indomitable; I thought they made him look like a twat. As usual he had matching running shorts, top and trainers, all Adidas to trick people into thinking they sponsored him.

We trotted down the farm path, jogging so slowly that it reminded me of competitions the children have to see who can cycle the slowest without falling off. The tiredness from the afternoon's bike ride and the 60 minute morning run left my legs. The dirt track was sticky from the storm. Huge clods of clay clung to my trainers but I felt so light that I bounded on as if held up by strings. After a couple of kilometres the pace picked up. Alfred and Moses continued talking to each other and Mike laughed at the appropriate place to show he wasn't getting breathless, but they were speaking in Kiswahili and there was no way he could understand.

Joyce was listening to her iPod so I didn't speak to anyone. You might ask if I find it boring to run without music. But your question wouldn't really make any sense to me. I'm neither bored nor excited when running. It is something else all together. I don't know many proper runners who train whilst listening to music. There's something sacrilegious about this, like checking text messages in a church or mixing malt whisky with coke. The very act seems like a distraction, preventing you from hearing your own rhythm, finding your own mantra.

When we got to the bridge at the bottom of the hill we stopped to let Mike and Moses zero their watches. Everyone waited while Mike tightened the band on his heart rate monitor and checked that his pedometer was clipped securely.

"I'm not doing it," Joyce stated, picking red clay from her ironed hair. No one asked her why but she added, "It's too boring." She sat on the side of the bridge, occasionally throwing bits of dried grass into the river and muttering, "Too boring for words."

The rest of us lined up. After the bridge came a farm track that was straight and not too steep for 100 metres, then a hairpin and a further 200 metres, with the gradient increasing all the time. A real lung burner even when not at altitude.

"Are we ready to go, Inspector Gadget?"

Mike nodded but didn't smile.

"Ok," said Moses putting his hand to his watch. "Go."

The boys sprinted off, splattering us with rust coloured earth. It reminded me of doing speed sessions on dry cinder football pitches in Scotland. I kept with Faith and Sylvia. Trying to regain speed after the bend I felt like I'd been winded but concentrated on using my arms and staring at the piece of ground three steps in front of me.

"Bit fast," Moses said, and I wasn't sure if this was a statement or a question. From this elevated point I spied kilometres of lush rolling fields, huts dotted here and there, labourers returning home along the meandering road, women bent double carrying massive loads of kindling. Man, it was too much. I suffered a moment of terrible panic. What on earth was I doing sprinting again and again up a hill in Africa? How had life deposited me here, doing this absurd thing, when there were so many other things that needed doing?

I joined the others jogging back to the start, searching for a look of uncertainty on any of their faces. But they all seemed pretty sure that this was the one thing they should be doing at that exact moment. Sometimes people laughed and joked at the start of a session but there wasn't much chat amongst us. At the bottom we grouped, turned and did it again. I blazed the first four efforts but by the fifth was having to dig deep just to stay close to the two girls. By the sixth my hands were on my knees and I was wheezing desperate breaths before standing dizzily and staggering down the hill. I had barely recovered by the seventh, and fell badly behind. By this stage I had stopped looking at the others for confirmation that they were suffering. As I jogged down to the start I saw Joyce sneering at me. She had tied the front of her T-shirt in a knot and was combing her hair with her fingers. Seven down, three to go, I told myself. You do these next two and you've broken this session. The last one will look after itself.

I dug my finger nails into the palms of my hand as Moses said, "Go." I had better acceleration than the Kenyan girls and reached the bend first. Faith pushed on and we ran elbow to elbow for the last stretch, but she made no great effort to pass me. Everyone stood with their hands on their knees dragging in the thin air that seemed to snare and tear over my teeth. The taste was somewhere between licking batteries and the aftertaste of cheap mint choc-chip ice cream.

Moses said, "Let's nail these last two," in his best Canadian college freshman voice and Mike smiled but looked sick. As I jogged down the hill beside him, he didn't even tell me about his pulse rate or average times.

"Only two to go," he said. I was about to reply with something encouraging before realising he was talking to himself. The ninth effort was a total mess. The girls got away from me and I lost concentration so badly that I started watching the boys at the front. As usual Alfred, who had no watch or pulse rate monitor, had judged the session perfectly. While the others were flailing, he was blazing over the last few metres, head held high, form unreal.

The last effort was the usual balls-out race. I grimaced, fighting for breath; my lips stuck to my dusty teeth. I was on my knees at the end, pulse pounding in my temples.

"Come on. Up!" Mike ordered, offering me an arm, knowing it's better to not lie down. "Your legs have gone green. That's lactic acid," he explained.

"I'm certainly feeling some of that."

For a ludicrous moment I thought he was going to hug me but instead he patted my back. It was only then that I read the front of his T-shirt. *Trample the weak, hurdle the dead.* Mike had a big collection of running T-shirts with twisted motivational expressions like this.

Faith and Sylvia nodded to indicate I had done well. I grinned like crazy at everyone. What wouldn't I have given for a hug? Mike grinned back at me.

"My pulse was up to 222 at the end of that." He said. "One minute recovery and it's down to 192."

"Is that a good thing?"

"It's much higher than my previous maximum heart rate. But I don't know if that's a result of training at altitude or an indication that I'm coming down with something. It might just be a problem with my heart rate monitor." He started fiddling with the device. "I'll check it again in a minute."

We decided to run back along the railway line. It was a little further but allowed us to shout on Joyce and watch her annoyance at having to run up the hill. The boys were chatting away, full of post-session euphoria. Mike would attribute it to endorphins but for me it was a glorious awareness of my body, a blessed tiredness, a confirmation that I was alive: and a sense of relief.

Joyce ran ahead with the boys and said something that cracked them up. I ran with Faith and Sylvia, watching their stork thin legs, their feet barely touching the ground, their upper bodies poised and regal as they covered the ground.

Back at the farm house we showered quickly in cold water piped directly from a well 30 metres under the house. The only way I could endure it was to step right in and make sure all my skin was touched by the icy spray, that there were no hot parts under my arms or between my legs.

The dining room was big enough for the twenty or so orphans that the Ks had living with them to eat dinner together. There was one long table covered with a transparent plastic sheet which protected the checkered table cloth from stains. The walls were bare, apart from a faded print of Da Vinci's Last Supper. When it was only adults eating, the room seemed quiet,

Dinner was the usual bowl of rice and over boiled vegetables cut into tiny perfect cubes. Joyce covered her plate in salt then, once the food was served, drenched everything in tomato ketchup she had brought back from Scotland. Mike always looked on appalled and talked at great length about the problems she'd have with her heart but only when Joyce had stopped playing with her food and left the room. At the other end of the table Joyce's mother, Gladys, sat with two big bosomed Africans and a white woman who seemed old and abandoned like a shoe by the roadside. The African women were wrapped in crazy colourful dresses and headscarves. They were loudly discussing and dismembering the day's newspapers in loud voices.

The newspapers in Kenya were written in this real old-fashioned English and were full of stories about politics. This wouldn't have meant a shit to me in Britain but I'd seen enough out here to know how heated the people were getting about this election. Every day we saw things on the street that shocked me, things that needed to be stopped.

"Who's the woman?" I mouthed.

Joyce grinned and loudly answered, "Bunyala Zandra."

Her mum shot her a fierce look. Joyce got to her feet, clattering her plate and cutlery. She said, "You can't finish either, bad, wasn't it?"

"You have surrendered?" asked one of Gladys's friends.

"The food has defeated me," she answered sarcastically.

"Remember," her mother warned, "even a lion will eat grass when there is no meat."

"Coming?"

I pretended not to hear her and stayed at the table to try and distance myself from her behaviour. Gladys's friend was telling the others about a speech one of Odaiga's supporters had made in Eldoret that day.

"There was a riot, some protesters were badly beaten, some might even have been shot," I blurted.

The women turned and stared at me. Outside, children sang in the play area, and a dog barked in the distance. "There was no riot," asserted the same woman. "And if the young lady witnessed the police using force then I would suggest that what she saw were not protesters but criminals."

Their conversation resumed. I tried to follow their words

but they made no sense to me and for a moment I thought my brain had snapped. This had been happening a lot recently. Mike said it was a side effect of the anti-malarial drugs we were taking but nonetheless I was relieved when I realised they'd switched from English to Kiswahili.

"But, I filmed it happening on my camera. It was definitely a political protest and the police just attacked them."

Gladys glowered at me. "Filming the police is illegal."

"What they were doing was illegal."

"That is not news to me."

"It might be news to the rest of the world."

"The world is past caring. If I were you, I would get rid of that film now. Pretend it never happened, pretend these things don't happen."

There was a silence until Mike clattered his cutlery. "Come on, you can help me with my tests."

I never helped Mike do his blood tests or fill in the charts recording haemoglobin levels and all that weird shit that I didn't understand. Instead I took out my journal and started describing the day's events.

"Are you logging your times from the hill session?" he asked.

"Not exactly."

The women were murmuring in Kiswahili. I felt sure they were talking about me.

It was the white woman who finally signaled for my attention.

"Gladys tells me you've been here three months and would like to see a bit more of the country before leaving."

I'd never expressed these sentiments but they were true enough.

"I work for a charity," Zandra continued in a Mid-Atlantic drawl. "We give talks in remote villages to try and educate women about their rights. We're going to a village near Mount Elgon tomorrow. If you and your friend want to join us we'll be leaving at 7."

"For real? That'd be sweet."

"We could organise a trip for you to the area near the Kitum Cave… this is an area few tourists see."

"Well, we're all about getting off the beaten track."

The woman peered at me. "What have you done to your ears?"

"It's called gauging. It's becoming fashionable back in Britain but I've been doing it for years."

"I see."

"Of course it all started out here," I began, but she had turned back to the others.

The conversation returned to Kiswahili, so I padded out to the porch. The sun was setting. In the distance a few of those broccoli shaped trees were silhouetted against the sky. Two sapling-thin shimmers of smoke from where people were making fires grew tall before disappearing in the darkness. Moses leant against the wooden railing, staring furiously at the horizon. We listened to the insects in the fields as the yellow-orange horizon shifted shades like a speeded-up film of a bowl of mangos molding.

"I think I'd go crazy living in a place where the sun comes and goes at the same time all year."

"I think I am going crazy living in a place with no reception," Moses replied, shaking his mobile phone at the sky.

"Can you not try the landline?"

"Have you seen anyone try the landline? It's down, same as the internet. Every year, they put telephone lines up along the road to Eldoret. Every year the people cut the poles down. They strip the cables for copper wire that they make into jewellery and turn the wood into charcoal. See those trees over there? That used to be a forest. All of this did before it was cut down and turned into charcoal." He tried his mobile again before saying, "My father likes to say that we have not inherited this land from our ancestors; rather we have borrowed it from our children. If that is the case then I wonder what we will have left them."

He turned and went into the house. The camera hung heavily around my neck. Resisting the temptation to watch the horror I had captured on it, I closed my eyes and listened to the invisible insects, insistent as a detuned radio crackling with static.

Chapter Three

I had run 12km easy, done 300 lower abdominal sit-ups, 150 press ups and eaten two bowls of sweetened porridge all before 6.45 am. I sat in the Ks' big sitting room surrounded by glass cases full of trophies and medals and, feeling like a king. On the walls were photos of K being presented with awards by other legendary Kenyan runners such as Kip Keino and Mike Boit. Other photos had been taken at black tie events, where he stood with the likes of McEnroe, Senna, Pele. My resting pulse was totally normal as I sat amongst these greats. This, I thought, was exactly the type of room I would have in my house at the end of my career.

I would have liked some more porridge but the little kids were having their breakfast and some of them ate with their mouths open. Although it was never mentioned, it was obvious that most of them were Aids orphans. The reason I didn't want to be at the table wasn't because I thought you can contract HIV by eating with people who are infected. That was probably why Kirsten thought I wasn't there. But the truth was, I couldn't understand how these little bursts of energy with their shiny teeth and perfect skin could be carrying something that would kill them. I never felt comfortable around children, anyway. Kirsten would be there rubbing heads and tying shoes, acting like she was Princess Diana.

After gulping down a multivitamin and iron supplement I went over to the TV, stacked around which were a dozen or so VHS- videos featuring races from the 1980s. I slotted a tape labelled *The Home Straight* into the machine and flopped back on the couch. The video whirled, white UFO blobs sped across the black screen to be interrupted by the classic Grandstand theme and some dated graphics. I felt calmly excited, the way I imagined a soldier might in past times when he heard military tunes. The commentator was the late and much-loved Jim Harrison, Kirsten's grandfather; a man who at the time was described as The Voice of Athletics. His warm, rough Yorkshire accent generously attempted to add gravitas to the spectacle of the speed walk – a hundred or so men wiggling their way from the stadium like a fire alarm had gone off at a Kylie concert. Shots of the competitors in tight shorts, sunglasses and constipated looks of consternation were lovingly juxtaposed with clips of female shot putters, pug faced and purple haired as if they'd all been assembled by one unimaginative ham-fisted child.

The coverage of the 10,000 metres only showed the last two laps. Jim's voice had risen an octave and was picking up pace along with the athletes. The leading group had by this stage stretched out to single file, the gaps between the athletes growing, until those at the back were dropped. K, who came second and was by this stage world famous, was not a graceful runner. He leant slightly forward his arms circling far out to his sides as if they were keeping him balanced rather than propelling him forward. Jim Harrison remarked as always that K had developed this style from running to school with a bundle of books under his arm. The distance he ran and number of books he carried grew throughout his career and you could tell that the commentator would have liked to add some details about fighting lions or being chased by cattle thieves as being part and parcel of a typical Kenyan child's journey to school.

K in his prime sported a not inconsiderable moustache and was a good 10 to 15 kilos lighter than the man I'd glimpsed twice on the farm. Like most great runners there was a look of exaltation on his face, an agonised moment of revelation as he came close to breaking point. When he ran round the final bend he lapped an athlete in a British vest who stepped onto the second lane to let him past. The British athlete kept up for a few metres, then looked like he said something. The British athlete was Kirsten's dad: my coach. He still has his chiseled features and floppy hair and races a couple of ultra-marathons every year. Seeing him on the monochrome screen, I experienced the mix of emotions that I imagine many old Russians feel when watching film reels of Stalin. I rewound the video and watched the overtaking section a couple more times. I tried to lip read what he had said. When Kirsten was younger he used to jog round the side of cross country courses for the whole race never once letting up: "Time to pick up the pace," "You're better than this," "Lets step it up a gear," "You can catch her." It got to the stage where other runners' parents started to complain. Only when Kirsten dropped out of a race she was winning, with the words, "You've beaten them, they're finished," ringing in her ears and the ears of the other runners did he stop his barrage of encouragement.

Generally I've got no respect for people who say things when being overtaken but maybe at the Olympics, when you've already been lapped, it's different. In any case the camera only lingered on him for this brief moment. His father, the famous commentator, didn't even mention his name.

Kirsten came into the room and saw the race on the screen. A look of annoyance flashed across her face and I felt I'd been caught peeping at something personal and embarrassing. It must be weird hearing your dead grandfather's voice every time archived races are shown. I wanted to ask if she knew what Mr Harrison had said. Instead I told her, "It's your dad's race from the Olympics," as if that wasn't obvious. "Do you want to watch it from the start?"

"Nah, let's scoot."

We went out to the Range Rover where the woman with a name like a Sci-fi heroine or someone you receive Spam emails about Viagra from was waiting with her nest-like hair, Maasai jewellery and clothes that would be considered loud for a woman half her age back home.

The Westerners who actually lived out here seemed to have become either ultra-conservative, dressed like extras in Out of Africa, or had totally let themselves go and started dressing like postcard Kenyans, refusing to say hello or so much as acknowledge the existence of another white person even when they met you in the most off-the-beaten-track places. This lady had clearly fallen into the second of these two categories.

"Hello, I'm Zandra Lillia," she said, unwrapping her words. "Nice to meet you." Her Kenyan driver was playing Kiswahili rap on the radio whilst occasionally shouting out lines at imaginary homies or hoes in the field. Zandra seemed to have developed a capacity for ignoring this behaviour. "All set?" She asked as we loaded ourselves in the back. She tossed an old half-unzipped holdall on to the seat between us. I could see it contained an enormous purple dildo – not something I'd ever seen mentioned as an essential item to pack for a trip into the African outback. I decided to look out the window, hoping it wouldn't start buzzing or twirling or anything like that to draw attention to itself.

Zandra's driver accelerated away while leaning into the backseat saying, "My name's Ezekiel but you can call me E-Zee." He then insisted on doing one of those elaborate handshakes, his road rough palms slipping and gripping mine in an agony of confusion. Once done with this, he found other excuses to avoid watching the road, such as tuning the radio, peeling the leaves from a cob of sweet corn and checking his reflection in the mirror. "Look," he said pointing at a burnt out and overturned jeep that we passed everyday when running, "this car has beat the corner for speed and now it is lying with its legs in the air." Kirsten giggled and E-Zee laughed too, mistakenly thinking that she was amused by this sight. As we sped round another corner a group of skeletal cattle slouched into view and he brought the Range Rover to a skidding halt.

"Tha muthafuckas," he said, making his hand into an

imaginary gun and aiming it at the first of the animals. "Tha muthafuckas, don't know when to give up." The lead cow lifted its head, its tail languidly whipping flies from its rear. A boy no more than eight years old rushed at the animals, cracking a frayed rope over their backs and shouting angrily. The cows trotted from the road, obedient and patient as parents to a demanding child. The boy held them back until we had passed his sack cloth slip flapping in the breeze. He watched after our car, practising a couple of whips, loud as a gunshot salute.

"Poor things," Kirsten said. "This is a hard country on animals."

"It's not easy on humans either," Zandra added.

"Of course, that's true but I mean you wouldn't want to come back as a Kenyan cow."

"Come back?"

"Yeah, you know, be reincarnated." Kirsten paused and I felt myself blushing for her.

"Listen honey, you live, you die, and that's that. There's enough to worry that pretty little head of yours about in this life without getting too upset about coming back as a cow."

Concerned that Kirsten was about to launch into a potentially embarrassing argument I asked, "What would you like to be reincarnated as?"

Kirsten looked at me to see if I was joking and after some lip chewing consideration answered, "A Kobe cow. Have you heard of them? They're a breed of pedigree livestock in Japan that live on premium beer and are massaged three times a day. That sounds alright to me."

"But you'd end up being eaten by some Japanese Salary man."

"Well I'd be reincarnated as something else by then."

"Another type of cow?"

"Probably I'd have done my time as being a cow."

I decided to shut up, realising that the other two could hear us, although E-Zee was fiddling with the radio which was making a noise like children tearing open well wrapped presents.

"It is a shame and a pity," he announced. "The people in this part of the country cannot even get good radio reception. What a life," he said before switching off the stuttering hip hop. "Man, they don't even rap in English this far down the road."

E-Zee grinned at me in the mirror and chucked a see through plastic bag full of leaves onto my lap.

"What's this?"

"This is khat, man. Put it in your mouth and it gives up its goodness."

"Sorry, I'm not accustomed to eating leaves. They probably won't agree with my stomach"

"You don't eat them," E-Zee laughed.

Kirsten took the bag from me and gave it a good look. "I've heard of this stuff. You just chew it, right?"

"That's right. Take ten or twelve leaves and chew. It's fresh *and* fine."

Kirsten did as he said and pulled a face at me. "It's organic," she said.

"The leaves are probably filthy or maybe cleaned in dirty water. Spit it out."

"I cleaned them myself," said Zandra in a sing-song voice. "They're not dangerous."

"Go on, you have to try some of the local customs."

"How do you know it doesn't show up in drugs tests?"

"Have you ever heard of some African leaves showing up in drug tests?"

"Maybe this is their secret?"

"What secret?"

"The secret to their running success."

Kirsten snorted. She had bits of green paste and half-chewed leaves over her teeth.

"What does this stuff actually do?" She asked between chews.

"It's an appetite suppressant, but also helps you concentrate and it's a bit of a stimulant as well. All things to all men," Zandra announced. "Some scientists even believe in can be beneficial when fed to working animals."

We continued rocking and rolling, the Kitale Road taking us ever higher to a place where the air was thinner and the roadside shacks poorer, and where the children were wide eyed at the sight of us. E-Zee slipped a tape from his shirt pocket and into the cassette player. He whistled through a big gap in his teeth and improbably, monstrously, Phil Collins' 'Easy Lover' blasted from the loud speakers.

"Before you know it you'll be on your knees," he wailed tunelessly. He gave me a cheesy smile that made me shudder deep inside.

"You knows it man!"

Kirsten whooped and threw herself across the backseat laughing, so that her short blonde hair touched my right thigh. She lay there giggling and I could tell from the angle she was lying that she must be able to see the giant dildo in Zandra's bag. She looked up at me while slipping her hand in the bag. I felt a tightening in my Khaki shorts as she moved her hand as if fondling the thing.

"She'll take your heart but you won't feel it," E-Zee mournfully sang. I felt like I'd fallen into a warped musical. I coughed to clear my throat and to signify that I'd had enough of her nonsense. She rolled her head up my leg like I was a pillow. Flustered, I checked the altimetre on my watch. We had just reached a height of over 3000 metres above sea level. I for one had never been so high. E-Zee turned the volume right up and started singing along with Phil Collins and rolling his shoulders in a way that could not be conducive to good driving. "We're over 10,050 feet above sea level," I spluttered, but no one was listening.

Once Phil Collins was finished and Kirsten was sitting upright with her seat belt on like a responsible adult, Zandra decided to regale us with the story of her life. She was 55 and had been living in Kenya for 20 years. In the past she had a husband

and two children who all lived in North Carolina – or, at least, that was where she had left them. She still wrote Christmas cards every year but never provided them with a return address. That was all we needed to know about that.

She started telling us about her mission, narrating her life like she was a character in some nineteenth century story.

"But what about diseases or accidents?" I asked. "Living out here this long can't be easy."

It transpired she had come down with Dengue Fever in Mombasa, malaria in Malarkos and yellow fever in Kerio Valley. She had been bitten by two strays, injured in three car crashes and cursed by witch doctors in some villages and accused of being one in others. She had twice been medivacced: once to Dubai, which she recommended, and once to South Africa, which she did not. She told us that on one of these trips she believed she was an angel and was on her way to heaven. Then she told us that she worked for a Christian charity doing God's work even though she hadn't believed in him for years.

I interrogated her closely, making sure Kirsten was listening and understanding that here in front of us was evidence of what this country could do to a human being.

I remembered that Joyce had called the woman Bunyala Zandra, which she had explained meant something like woman from the outback and had not been intended as a compliment. I always got a feeling at the Ks that Gladys and the older women felt sorry for Zandra. She had a well scrubbed face and wore basketball trainers with her African dress. She walked on the heels of the trainers like she had corns or was afraid of disturbing people. Her face remained over-animated, agitated as if she doubted that her knowledge of the language we all used allowed her to express everything she wanted to say.

"Did you get rabies when you were bitten by the dogs?" She shook her head. "That's a pity. I've already spoken to people who'd caught those other diseases but it would be great to talk to someone who had actually recovered from rabies."

She seemed not to hear me and replied, "If a stone hits the egg, alas the egg. If the egg hits the stone still alas the egg." I nodded and looked thoughtful. "That's a Kenyan proverb," she added.

We drove on in silence, passing men carrying great loads on their backs and women with babies slung across the front of their chests, held safely there by colourful shawls. There seemed to be no reason for these people to be walking that road far from any settlements.

Then Kirsten shouted, "Antelopes!"

Straining out of her window I saw a group shimmering through the long grass.

"Stop the car," she yelped at E-Zee.

"They're only antelopes. Where you're going there is much more to see than antelopes." He foraged in the plastic bag and crushed a couple more leaves into his mouth. Whether the khat was helping him concentrate or he was seeing some complex and unsettling patterns on the tyre-scarred road was unclear, but he had stopped twisting round and now drove with his fat nose almost touching the windscreen.

"You've just entered Elgon national park," Zandra explained. "If you're lucky you'll see monkeys, lots of monkeys and elephants even."

Eventually a gigantic billboard reminding us to *Enjoy Coca-cola*, rusty and looking like a militia had used it as target practice, appeared over the scrub. Then came a few corrugated sheds, with many more people milling about than it seemed could possibly live in the few dwellings. We stopped in front of a concrete breeze block building painted yellow and called The Obama Café. The arrival of a car – and a car containing three white people – created a rustle of excitement and the usual throng of kids pressing their pale palms against the Range Rover's windows. We managed to climb out, and bought some Obama mango juice, which, though very good, had probably not been officially endorsed by the man many people were predicting would be the next president of America.

Zandra met some women and there were suddenly dozens of chugging hands, *Jambos*, bright smiles and Old Testament names.

"Come, now now," said a man whose big round face, moustache and AK-47 suggested he was in charge, "you will want something to bite."

He took us to a place called The Little Lambs School. As it was a Saturday neither children nor lambs were having lessons. We were given some plastic cups containing sweetened ugali, the same mucus-thick porridge that I'd had for breakfast and which we ate at least once a day. I got out my anti-septic wipes and cleaned the rim of the cup. I tried to pass them to Kirsten but she ignored me. I was also worried about the hygiene of the people who had prepared the ugali, but wasn't sure how I could refuse.

"Any news of the election?" the man asked Zandra.

She looked at us before replying in Kiswahili. I was still hungry from the morning's training and had a second bowl.

Zandra led us into the school's one big classroom; there was only one small window and it was cathedral cold behind the thick walls. There was an embarrassing scene as a heavily pregnant woman with a club foot and another woman who could have been her grandmother tried to make us take their chairs. The old woman pawed at my arm with her crustacean rough palms. She had a face full of sacrifice, creased and cracked as a sandal's sole.

Conversation became whispered behind hands, messages were sent in wide eyes, and there were small squeals as Zandra placed her holdall on the table at the front. News had obviously travelled from village to village – here was the woman with the purple plastic penis. Children's snub noses smeared against the window and the official-looking man beckoned Kirsten and me to come with him. Zandra was taking packets of condoms from her bag and handing them out amongst the women. Some shrieked and others clapped their hands but most were quiet, staring at the bag as if it were a magician's hat. As we went outside the children chinning up on the window sill leapt down and ran away.

"As for me, I am Jonah," he said by way of introduction. "I am a park ranger." We shook hands and I stared at the most impressive pair of nostrils I'd ever seen. What wouldn't a runner give to have nostrils like that? We wandered back to the Range Rover and got in to find E-Zee munching away at a huge pasty ball of khat.

"Not only is this an unpleasantness for the eyes," said Jonah, "but it is reprehensible for a man's moral being."

E-Zee decided not to get into an argument, which seemed like a wise decision considering the rifle balancing between Jonah's legs. We drove off accompanied by an explosion of screams and whistles from the school room telling us that the purple penis had finally been produced.

"Where are we going again?" I asked once we were five minutes from town.

"Oh, you'll see, we have a super surprise for you," Jonah answered, words which, if not worrying enough, were accompanied by villainous hand rubbing and a hacking laugh.

We drove up a grass track, then through undergrowth that surely no vehicle had passed. The gun was the real problem for me. I couldn't stop looking at the black polished metal, butt fixed with masking tape, and a rainbow coloured strap that I was sure had been appropriated from some hippy's acoustic guitar. Jonah kept moving it about, first on his lap, then with the butt on the floor. I realised that my interest was making him nervous. I felt like a young boy understanding the etiquette of public urinals for the first time.

"How's that khat stuff working out for you?"

"Oh, it's nothing really. Just like a couple of strong coffees."

"You ought to be careful with that type of stuff."

"We'll see."

"Are the young people in the back still very ok?" asked Jonah

"Mighty ok," Kirsten improvised.

"Right, we can stop here Ezekiel. Can you pick me at three? Yes, from this spot?"

"Are you sure this is safe?"

"Oh yes, this is the safety place. I only take this gun for precaution, so that you don't need to worry your heads off." Jonah spread his arms out to the rolling vista before us. "This is Africa," he enthused. "I organise trips for the little tourists who come here and they tell me, 'this is the real Africa.' "

We scrambled up thick grassy banks, monkeys chattering and disturbing branches in far off trees, always too quick for us to see. A group of children in baggy chinos and office shirts hanging down past their knees appeared and jogged around us like some strange bodyguard. They began singing and within minutes Kirsten joined in as if she knew all the words. Soon she was teaching them Kumbaya, the hokey kokey, all her favourites. The children translated the words into something which probably made far more sense to them than the originals did to me. Some words sounded rude and made them spin about with laughter. All this disturbance was not helping us see any wildlife but I didn't complain. We were in a different part of the country from the agricultural area where we had been living, and I kept seeing snakes petrifying into branches, spiders scuttling off as leaves.

As we climbed higher, I started to feel breathless, and was relieved to hear the noise of water dropping from a great height competing with the clamouring of monkeys and the censorious *hush* of wind in the trees. We clambered over some rocks and there in front of us were great cliffs, shaggy with moss and ferns.

"This is Mount Elgon?"

"This is all Mount Elgon. Look," said Jonah, "elephant dung."

"There are elephants here?"

"Probably not until nightfall. Soon we will see more of their work." The children suddenly and without warning ran away. I watched until they disappeared amongst the trees. Jonah noticed my unease and said, "This is a lonely part of the world. But beautiful, no? It is the hope of our people that tourists will flock here as they do in The Maasai Mara."

We walked towards a cliff where water splattered onto rocks below. "Here we see the entrance to the famous Kitum cave; you could fit three of your Wembley Stadiums in there. They were made by elephants over thousands of years. See the scars on the rock. These are from elephant tusks. They come here to dig the salt from the rock. At certain times of the year their diets are, how do you say it? Yes, deficient in salt. This is an elephant salt mine. You will tell the people of Great Britain and Northern Ireland about this place and they will come in their thousands."

"How do the elephants know?" Kirsten mumbled, slipping down to the cave's entrance and tracing a groove in its side.

"Me, what I know is all types of animals come here for the salt. Antelopes and zebras included. And of course they are followed by the predators and the predators are followed by the scavengers."

"What sort of predators?"

"Certainly leopards. This is a great place for seeing animals, especially when the night falls. In the future we hope to have viewing stations and, God-willing, binoculars."

"But we're not staying here till night fall. We have to get back. Do some training."

Jonah tutted. "This is a shame and a pity."

I stood as close to the man with the gun as was decent. Kirsten was meanwhile hopping from one foot to another. Leaning into the dark of the cave, she shouted, "Jambo, is anyone in?" I wanted to tell her to come back from there but the constant torrent of water made voices seem insignificant.

"What was the cave's name again?"

"Yes, this is the Kitum Cave."

"I've heard that name before."

"I said it was famous."

"But there are no tourists here."

"Aren't we lucky? Maybe you know the caves from one of your BBC documentaries. There was a book by some American, who had never even been here, full of inaccuracies that left people disinclined to visit." I tried to ask a question but he continued, "Also some claim that this is the treasure cave at the end of King Solomon's Mines." I laughed, sure I'd read of at least three other places with similar claims made for them. "Certainly it is a treasure trove for people who have come seeking ivory. Many elephants have fallen and died in the chasms at the back of the cave. Others the hunters simply shot."

There was no sun down there and I was getting wet from the waterfall's spray.

"It's becoming cold," I said, but Jonah was smiling at the spot where Kirsten had been standing.

"The young lady appears to have ventured into the cave. It would be wise if you could collect her."

I looked at his fat sweaty face, all nose and nostrils. "This cave is in a film, isn't it? Two tourists caught The Marburg Virus here."

"That film was nothing but common lies and scaremongering of the very worst kind. An American writes junk and you believe him and not me, this place is safe I tell you." Jonah rambled on but I was already running down the bank, jumping from rock to rock, agile, lithe, superheroic. Inside the Kitum cave the dark swaddled me. The noise of the waterfall was replaced by the distant screeching of bats and a sound like the flapping of abandoned tents.

The cave, if I remembered the film correctly, was believed to contain a natural reservoir for the Marburg Virus, which many believed was carried by bats. Like Ebola it had a biosafety level 4 rating, meaning there was no effective treatment; people infected died from multiple organ failure, haemorrhaging from orifices, that sort of thing. As an adolescent I had spent even more time

41

reading about the effects of these diseases than I had looking at photos showing the symptoms of tropical STDs.

I shuffled forward. The cave wasn't wet or claustrophobic, and I felt no need to keep ducking for fear that winged things with hooks and teeth might touch my head. Instead I sensed the majesty of the place: it was somehow larger than the entire world outside. The immensity drew me in, that and knowing Kirsten was in there, possibly stuck or injured or in need of being saved. I crept forward, telling myself I was not a coward.

A hysterical, high, and mirthless laugh stopped me in my tracks. I remembered Jonah mentioning scavengers and at once thought *hyena*. I crept across the invisible floor, my hands held out in front trying to persuade anything out there to halt. Kirsten was somewhere in here and the obvious thing was to shout, but I had a dream-like certainty that I couldn't produce a sound: that my tongue, lips, throat were dry as blocks of salt.

There in that smothering darkness I knew what it must be like to leave your body. My feet tested the ground beneath them to make sure I didn't drop into some elephants' graveyard, and my hands trembled in anticipation of hot sticky teeth.

I stumbled on a rock or bone and my hands touched flesh. Warm, standing, still, there. I heard an intake of breath, rubbed the downy hairs on her arms and hugged her. We stood like that, her wet face on my chest, conscious only of the other one breathing. Then a bellow like an elephant or some ancient beast trumpeting the birth of a new disease made us race back into the sunlight.

Chapter Four

On the way home we were caught in the same storm that brought drama and a sense of relief to every afternoon. We sat in the back seat listening to the downpour drumming on the roof. But not even the grumble of thunder outside made me feel happy to be in the Range Rover. My leg jittered, the inside of my bones felt cold and I understood that I would never feel so utterly alone as I had in that cave. Occasionally we passed clusters of traditional wooden huts, but saw no people. There was a feeling of 'heritage centre', of something authentically reconstructed but not lived in. I leaned out of the window. The road was slightly elevated and we could see mile upon mile of hilly husbanded land. I was sure that if I could spot one person carrying firewood or herding goats through that desolation then I would scream at E-Zee to stop and beg that they abandon me. I found Mike's talk of altitude difficult to comprehend; we were thousands of feet higher than the tallest mountains in Britain. Sometimes I imagined that we were on an enormous saucer of land, floating above the clouds, detached from the earth.

Zandra spoke enthusiastically about the afternoon's meeting and how Kenya could only prosper if the women had more power, how the pope was responsible for genocide because of his stance on condoms and that the only way to save Africa was to reduce the birth rate. These were all opinions and issues that I'd read lots about, and they must once have interested me. Now though, I couldn't think of anything to say. She could have been talking about the lifecycle of May flies for all I cared. Our silence didn't seem to bother her. She was like a preacher who didn't care if anyone was converted. On and on she went about marital rape, the rights of adopted female relatives, enforced female circumcision. Occasionally I'd punctuate her tirade with a, "Shocking, how terrible, ghastly," in that disapproving voice British people use to signify that it is not the subject matter that is ghastly but the fact that someone was bringing it up in company. I felt like a cold hearted bitch but couldn't stop myself.

"I can't believe you let that man take us there," Mike interrupted. "Have you got a headache?" He scrutinised me. "A headache is the first symptom of the Marburg virus."

E-Zee whistled through his teeth.

"The US army's infectious disease unit came to Mount Elgon decades ago to analyse the cave and checked thousands of local species to see if they carried the virus. They found nothing. The cave is safe and you were very rude to a man who has been my friend for twenty years and offered to take you on a tour out of the kindness of his heart. Jonah is an important man. He is certainly not used to a boy like you shouting at him and carrying on in a hysterical manner."

Silence followed this reprimand until Mike turned to me and asked, "Are you running?"

I thought for a moment that I might open my mouth and some primal booming sound would come from it, the kind of sound that might rend the skies or at least any bonds of friendship I had with Mike.

"Will the ground not be too sticky?" I said. My voice sounded flat like a recording on an old tape.

"It'll be far from perfect but I think good training for the Cross Countries in January."

I felt sick. January and February were when all the big races of the Winter Season took place. The National long and short course championship, The Celtic Games, The Europeans. In March The World Cross Country Championships were to be held at Holyrood, in Edinburgh. And so on, race after race: never stopping, winning one, making the team for another, all year long.

Most nights I dreamt about running over a barren Scottish hillside, my feet slipping and sticking in the snow. It was never clear who I was racing, since there was no one in front of me and, try as I might, I couldn't see anyone chasing me. But what was clear was my desperation. Even in the biggest races I'd never skittered across the ground with such a sense of panic. As I ran, a series of false summits came and went and I realised the end would never be in sight, that the race was over.

"My Achilles are a bit sensitive, so I'll probably give this one a miss."

Mike shrugged. "I'd like to run but I really do have a headache." He winced theatrically and started to massage his temple.

We drove on past more deserted huts. You should have seen me when we first arrived here, taking photos every time I passed one of these, every time I saw some exotic bird or street child in rags. Snap, snap, snap. Closing my eyes, I pretended to sleep. I needed to try and understand what had happened in the cave.

Mike was muttering about multi-organ dysfunction and liver failure and opening my eyes a little I could see him prodding his belly.

Standing in the mouth of the cave, breathing in that old air unsweetened by trees or breeze but only a distant tang of fermented bat shit, all I had wanted to do was enter. And once I was in, I'd been terrified, yes, of course: but also comforted. I felt that I could just sit there and hide. Be nurtured and fed by the beasts. Let people forget who I am. When Mike grabbed me I was sorry to be wrenched back into the real world.

At the ranch, there was no sign of the Ks so I hung around the kitchen scandalizing Agnes with my attempts to help her with the cooking. Mike went and got ready for his run. It was unusual for him to go anywhere alone and I could hear him doing drills between the farmhouse and orphanage, clearly hoping Moses or Alfred would appear. Then he was gone and

Agnes was fretting about where the others were and asking me whether she should just go ahead and feed the little ones first.

Agnes was a Maasai, which was pretty unusual in this part of Kenya. She was even taller than me, and totally flat chested. With her wiry hair cropped short, her hard angular face and her strong, sinewy arms she seemed asexual as a carving. What distinguished her as a Maasai was the jewellery she wore, the opaque bead necklaces and head bands, which made a sound like a box of rice shaking as she completed her many duties. But it was her ears that fascinated me most: the lobes were pierced and expanded over years to fit large circular earrings. I also wore jewellery that expanded the fistula in my earlobes and I was wearing silver flesh tunnel earrings about the diameter of a ballpoint pen. The ornaments that Agnes had worn must have been far bigger and I would have liked to have known how she had gauged such big holes and what materials she had used as jewellery. But I didn't ask; she never wore earrings anymore and her ear lobes now flapped about the side of her neck, stringy and misshapen like worms dried out on a pavement.

Agnes seemed to like me. We spent a lot of time together helping the children make bead necklaces and bracelets, which she sold at a market to the few tourists who passed through Eldoret. I had checked to see how much they sold for and was horrified to realise that 3 hours of my work resulted in a necklace worth about 10 pence. Of course the children with their thin fingers could make a lot more than this but they only worked until they got bored and when the weather was too bad to play outside.

I went through to help clear the table but they were midway through a game of Monopoly. Sammy, who had drunk the bubble liquid, was the banker and had clearly embezzled lots of money down his shorts. As usual no one had bought any streets, houses or hotels, content to simply pass Go, collect their £200 whilst trying to steal money from the banker when he wasn't looking. Edith, the only one who understood the rules, had thrown a tantrum because one of her sisters had hidden the Regents Park card, knowing that she was only interested in the green streets. Little Gideon had pinched all the houses from the box and had constructed an unpaid for skyscraper on Old Kent Road, but as yet no one had noticed.

A rustling of beads warned us that Agnes was at the door. The kids cleared up, quick as poker players round an illegal gaming table.

"What's all this evil doing in my dinner room?" asked Agnes, laughing as they presented their innocent faces. Dinner was served and *man* did they love their food! I never once saw any of them farming carrots around their plate. They ate the way they played Monopoly, thankful for what they had, fearful only of theft.

Joyce poked her head round the door and waved at me to follow. She had been at a friend's place and she had braided her hair and was wearing false talon-long nails and a clownish amount of make-up.

"Quick, we're not eating here," she said, ushering me out the door. I took one last look at the children, wishing that I could spend the night safely circling the familiar Monopoly board. .

I'd never been sure whether Joyce could legally drive. She was 17, so in Britain old enough, but as far as I knew she'd never taken any lessons. The first time we'd got in a car she'd told me that all it took was confidence: and Joyce certainly had that in spades. As we drove towards Eldoret we passed Mike, the back of his T-shirt and legs totally covered in mud, a look of contented concentration on his face.

That was the big difference between us; he actually enjoyed training, and not just the running part. For him making programmes, setting targets, all the diets and scientific paraphernalia seemed just as important. No doubt he was excited about what today's rise in altitude would have done to his blood iron count and of course he would be exalting in the fact that yet again he had put in more mileage than me. But he really loved running. You could see it in the way he walked up on his toes as though he was simply waiting – longing – for someone to say *"Go!"* We'd raced at the same meetings and trained on the same track since we were in primary school. He was always up for it, comparing times, competing, pushing until he became better.

My parents had dozens of newspaper clippings from events where he'd won the boys' race and I the girls'. People always talked about us in the same sentence, normally with words like potential, great futures, ones to look out for. It made me sick. None of them knew anything. Mike might make it but the odds of being selected for a senior Olympic or even Commonwealth team were pretty long. After that, the odds he'd do anything at a distance totally dominated by Africans were even longer. I knew my own future. Sometimes that made me feel tremendously and terribly powerful. I knew I was totally and utterly fucked. The great pressure was waiting to find out how long it would take everyone else to realise this.

Catching me looking at him in the wing mirror, Joyce said, "Fuck him." I smiled and she added, "I would."

Joyce was big into Reggae, mid-90s British Triphop and a lot of new Dubstep artists that I hadn't heard of. She was always fiddling with the car's tape player complaining that it didn't have enough bass. We stopped at a café on Malaba Road, next door to a sports shop that her father owned. I wondered if the famous man would be in, but Joyce showed no interest in showing face.

"Could we go to the internet café?" I asked, clutching my camera, whose guilty weight I'd been carrying since the riot.

"It shut an hour ago sunshine, we'll go tomorrow on the way home." She strode across the cracked and crumbling pavement in her heels, curling her lips as if she could smell something vaguely disgusting. I followed, feeling like a dowdy servant in my trainers, combats and oversized hoody,.

Our tribe of street children raced towards us, holding shoeboxes filled with packets of tissues and chewing gum.

"Hello tissue, hello fine, hello 10 shillings," they yelled at us.

Malpas was nowhere to be seen. They had a new leader who wore a denim jacket and a red cravat and looked a lot like a young Michael Jackson. He was not as forward as Malpas and instead stood a little apart from the others, a small smile for their desperation, showing off his dimples. It was crazy, but at the age of nine or ten he already knew that any foreign women would buy from him. As the others grappled at your sleeves shouting "mother, father, sister gone, you promised before," he swung on one foot and shrugged, embarrassed for their efforts.

"The boy with the Dundee United strip ... the orange top. Where is he?"

The cute kid blinked and nodded with friendly incomprehension. I bought a packet of tissues from him for 20 shillings – about 10 pence. Ridiculously overpriced everyone told me, but how could you haggle with street children? Mike had explained that buying at this price was all wrong as it encouraged the children to stick at selling these items since they could make more money off stupid tourists than they ever would from doing a proper job. Consequently, he said, they wouldn't go to school or contribute to the economy. But for me, in a city where even the best cafes and restaurants had toilets without any paper in them, they provided an invaluable service.

"We need to get some food in you girl, you are wasting away. Me, I think burgers and chips are the answer," insisted Joyce, pulling me away from the crowd.

"Me tomorrow, me tomorrow," they wailed.

The cute kid with the cravat said goodbye with his eyes and a mournful pursing of his lips, like some martyr whose greatest sorrow is for those who condemn him.

Joyce managed to persuade me to drink my first beer in weeks, a 330ml can of Tusker, black and yellow can with a picture of an elephant on the front.

Looking at the elephant, she smirked. "So you managed to survive Bunyala Zandra. Christ, I have no time for that woman.

She's always on at my mum with her politics and good works. Trying to improve the world. And then she does this big act of humility. You know, sleeping on the floor when there are spare beds or not taking showers when there's running water. Me, I piss on her piety."

"I'm just going to have some scrambled eggs," I said, "You know I don't eat meat."

"You don't know what you're missing. Look at all the condiments," she collected bottles of sauce and mustard from the counter. "I'm going to pinch the ketchup, I'm running out of the stuff."

The scrambled egg was greasy and rubbery but I managed to get most of it down. When Joyce went to chat up the guy at the bar I wrapped the two pieces of toast in a napkin and stuffed them in my pocket. I forked the rest of the scrambled egg to one side and waited for Joyce to come back.

"Wow finished already. Let's go." She gave me one of the carrier bags; both were full to bursting with beer cans.

"They do know we're coming?"

"Sure."

"And they know why we're coming?"

"Kirsten, girl, stop fretting. You've been there yourself. They're hardly going to run out of the stuff."

We drove out of Eldoret's sparse lights. We were heading for a place called Noah's Camp, a stop-off for Alternative Safaris, a place where western students or dropouts trundling down Africa, behaving as badly as possible for as little money as possible, could hang out for a couple of days. The campsite had ten pre-pitched Vango six-man tents that smelt deliciously of canvas. There was a big wood log hall and two marquees where travelers could eat, drink, listen to music and smoke. The smoking was the important bit. There was no-one called Noah.

Joyce and I didn't actually like each other and when we were running or travelling rarely spoke. At best it could be said that we shared a cynical solidarity based around the pressures of having fathers who expected us to be good at something they were great at. But mostly our relationship was based on a shared love of smoking gargantuan quantities of cannabis.

You will ask how does one of the best junior runners in the country get into something so obviously detrimental to their sport? I could blame Joyce. She introduced me to weed, returning from boarding school to stay at my parents' one half-term holiday when she was about 14 with a cigarette packet full of illicit weed and the possibility of secret rebellion, of sabotaging the person that everyone was expecting me to be. But let's face it, plenty of people I knew smoked dope, an occasional joint at a party or hanging around a bus stop after school. Some liked it or liked the idea of it, and for them it became a hobby, or even something that defined them. Most weren't that bothered one way or another. But none of these people were spending all of their money, in my case winnings from races, sponsorship deals or Athletic Federation grants, on buying ever-increasing, vacuum-packed plastic bags of the most pungent weed a teenage suburban girl is likely to get her sweaty mitts on.

Our headlights picked out the 'Noah's Camp' sign and the strange Totem poles that someone had carved in a time when such multi-eyed monstrosities existed. They gave me the fear; they and the thought we might be too late, that I wouldn't have the chance to fumigate my mind of the street children's faces.

Two Jeeps with South African registration plates were parked haphazardly, and thick voices chortled around the barbecue area. Occasional gargoyle-like faces dipped in and out of the firelight and I saw by their long matted hair that they were white Rastafarians, probably on some stupid pilgrimage to Ethiopia.

"Christ," I muttered to Joyce, "and I thought *I* was lost and confused."

In the log hall the three Kenyans who ran the place sat slumped, in deck-chairs, long limbs akimbo. "Jambo," they said, the greeting sounding masculine and profound.

"Jambo," we replied. I sat down next to the one who spoke

the best English and who the others called Django. This was clearly not his real name: when I called him it everyone laughed.

"How is it?" he asked.

"Very fine," I replied. "Listen, I filmed something with this camera. A protest actually. A boy I know, a Kenyan, was injured or killed. It's difficult to see on the camera but on a full screen it will be clear." I paused. "I think the police may have shot him."

Django nodded but his face was exhausted, his eyes barely open.

"I was wondering if you had any sort of internet connection that I could use to send these images to news agencies in Britain."

Joyce snorted. "Yeah, these guys are online. Why don't you use the computer next to the phone with a direct connection to the President of America?"

The others laughed and slouched back in their deck chairs. I'd known that they wouldn't have the internet, but still I resented Joyce for preventing me feeling less bad about myself.

Seven or eight candles stuck in whisky bottles, the distiller names obscured by thick manes of melted candle wax, gave an element of mystery to proceedings. In the middle of the room a white girl with matted hair twisted and twirled. When I say white, I mean white like a paracetamol and with the same sheen that you have on some pills to make them easy to swallow. The first time I had seen her she seemed to be part of a Dutch group of ornithologists who had landed in the camp by accident. The next time I thought she was with some American backpackers who actually turned out to be doing religious work - hanging about in strange parts of the world, spending most of their lives in matching suits, all wearing small name badges and hoping to find converts and biding their time until they could go back home and make a family. By the third visit I realised she belonged to no one. She wore a broad brimmed hat like an elderly person afraid of the sun. The rest of her clothes had a lost property look about them. She might have been with one or all three of the Kenyan men that ran the place, but they pretty much ignored her. There was a screen at one end of the hall on to which they may once have projected movies. She used to dance in front of this the snickering candle light casting her shadows.

Instead of movies the men generally played music. They had a big old ghetto blaster that played those compilation CDs of songs from the Sixties that are often sold in service stations back home. The girl jived to one hit wonders who were only on the album as they cost nothing in royalties. Songs that you know by artists you've never heard of but that still give you a sunbleached nostalgia for a time and place that was never, ever yours. The girl's dancing revolved around four stock moves and was always pretty enthusiastic. It didn't seem to matter whether the music was some slow folk song or an upbeat Motown number, the moves and the speed at which they were executed were exactly the same. But it was her face that fascinated me: A smile tugged at one side of her mouth as she stared at some insignificant chair leg or ash tray as if she had discovered its real purpose. Her eyes, the few times she let them glance my way, reminded me of ancient coins long lost beneath the ground. They must have sparkled once and even now with years of expert care could be restored to something beautiful again.

I had tried to talk to her but she shrank from me like a shy child.

"Drink," Joyce said, passing cans to two of the men. Django put up a hand to say *not me*. "I'm not asking, I'm telling." Joyce opened the beer with a spurt, licked the foam from her thumb and said, "Cheers."

"Afya," said the tallest of the men who was wearing a Vote Gore T-shirt.

The second man reached out and shook my hand even though we had met a couple of times before. Looking to the ceiling for inspiration he recited, "My names are Amos Ngugi, I hail from Eldoret and my digits are 0722457985. Furthermore my alma mater is Moi University."

"Hujambo," I replied, shaking his hand.

Django gave me his can and whispered, "I can't drink this." He stretched to open the battered old fridge and pulled out a Fanta.

"What's this?" Joyce asked.

"Django is a Muslim," explained Vote Gore. "I keep telling him, it's late, Allah is asleep but he don't listen."

They all laughed, including Django. "Maybe when it is after twelve, when I'm sure he is safe in bed."

"Fanta stands for what?" asked Vote Gore. I looked confused and he slurped loudly from his can.

"I don't think it stands for anything."

This was clearly the wrong answer. Vote Gore shook his head like I was a great disappointment and said, "Foolish Arabs Not Take Alcohol!" He slapped his hands on his thighs. "That is what it stands for. I thought this was well known." Django pretended to attack him and they ended up rolling on the floor covered in beer. Meanwhile the white girl did big fish, little fish, reach for the stars, while the Mamas and Papas sang *California Dreaming*.

Eventually I got tired of all the fooling around and gave Joyce what I hoped was a significant look. She raised her perfectly plucked eyebrows as if I was asking a great favour. After a while she must have popped the question for Vote Gore wobbled to his feet and walked like a man in leg irons out of the Hall. When he returned he was carrying a carrier bag full of sweet smelling marijuana. Skins and packets of shag appeared and the man started constructing, rolling, licking, picking runaway bits of tobacco off his tongue.

"I make it strong strong. Like your friend likes it." He thrust his chin in my direction.

As the joint was passed from hand to hand I ground my teeth, trying not to calculate how many tokes it was till my turn. Joyce even offered it to the dancing white girl which seemed totally unnecessary considering her perma-stoned state. In any case she batted the offered joint away, seemingly far more interested in re-enacting the life cycle of a butterfly to *We Gotta Get Out Of This Place*.

Finally Amos passed me the joint and I pretended to be uninterested, tapping the ash into an old beer can, fixing the roach. Then I placed the soggy paper to my lips and inhaled, ballooning my pure young lungs, hugging myself with my free hand, fingers fitting between my jutting rib bones. I let some smoke trickle out my nostrils but held most of it in. My fingers shook. I no longer cared if they were watching me, judging. The blunt crackled as some particularly pungent weed burnt. The smoke twined in creamy, loose pleats, then disappeared in frayed ends.

Two of the South African Rastas had sniffed us out and stood at the edge of the marquee, watching. A couple of joints were doing the rounds but although we were all aware that they were standing there no one invited them to join us. Eventually the dirtier of the two cleared his throat and spoke to Vote Gore in whimpering weedy Afrikaans. To my surprise he answered in their language, his voice sizzling and crashing. The South Africans took heart and starting negotiating. Vote Gore must have made a joke as one of them let out a shrill whinny of a laugh before clamping a hand to his face, coughing and chuckling gruffly. Joyce looked at them with disgust. It was only when they turned to leave that I realised that one of them was a woman. After they had gone Joyce sniffed the air in an exaggerated manner and everyone laughed except Django.

"Come," he said, "a hyena cannot smell its own stink."

We smoked some more and I sidled over to Vote Gore so that I could buy from him. The truth was I hated smoking in company. In Scotland this usually meant sitting in a room with idiots who had played Premiership Manager into the next century, had posters on their walls of toking aliens, believed every conspiracy theory going and treated me, a girl, as if I'd dropped in from another planet. These Kenyans weren't so bad. They switched into their own language, not Kiswahili or a tribal dialect, so Joyce told me, but Sheng, a patois spoken by young people that her mother forbade in their house. I liked the sound of their laughter and deep voices and the fact I was totally exempt from the conversation. Still, I wanted to smoke alone and, after uncrumpling myself, swayed to my feet mumbling the word 'toilet'. As I crossed the hall the dancing girl jerked as if someone had just grabbed her head, and mouthed along to The Beach Boys, "Where did your long hair go, where is the girl I used to know?" Then she was back to imitating a snake or a river or a person melting on the spot.

I rubbed my hand along my scalp, feeling the soft hair I'd allowed to grow to a length where it could almost be called pretty for the first time in years. I'd have to shave it off the moment I got home. I'd read that cannabis traces remain in hair for months, and as an athlete competing at the level I did, you had to expect all sorts of testing for illegal substances.

Outside, the night was so sodden with darkness that I doubted I could wade through it. We were just north of the equator so the constellations should have been familiar, but they were lost amongst a dizzying multitude of stars. Looking up there you could actually believe that the big bang was happening before your eyes.

I spat a rotten raisiny spit. The back of my throat felt singed by the harsh tobacco smoke. My tongue trawled across the back of furry teeth and rubbed against the roof of my mouth, rough like rind. I spat again but there was nothing there. My hands found the napkin wrapped toast in my pocket and I chewed it to a doughy ball, spreading the oozing butter around my dry mouth. I couldn't swallow. I bent over and let the masticated toast plop to the ground.

At our tent I struggled to convince my hands to stop stroking the rough hemp door ropes and instead try to untie them. Inside I put on my head torch and sat cross-legged with the bag of marijuana in my lap. At the last moment I had brought my second best vapouriser to Kenya and I carefully unpacked this. It had cost me $190. Vapourisers are perfect for someone like me. They heat the herb to a temperature where all you are inhaling are the psychoactive ingredients. Nothing burns and you're not rolling the drug in tobacco so you're not exposed to carcinogenic smoke. This is a great advantage when you're midway through a 10 x 400 metre session on the track. It is also incredibly, intensely efficient.

I plucked some buds and heated them in the machine's black body. It took longer than my best vapouriser which I had bought before the summer and has a Quartz Crystal heating element, four fan speeds and no plastic parts. Unfortunately it also looks like a weapon of mass destruction and would probably have caused major chaos with airport security. So I was back with this one, described in its advert as being *great for people on the go, ideal when driving or sailing*. It reached optimum temperature and I inhaled the smooth vapours, feeling as if I'd put my head round the door of a sauna. I took another hit, and then again and again until my body sagged and any movements my fingers made were fascinating and tarantula like. I felt moist, I kept thinking I might have pissed myself, but my hand told me I hadn't. *Man*, I smoked so much that I could no longer work the machine; so I crawled out into the camp's lush grass.

I tasted the wet from the afternoon's storm with my tongue, and ground my knees and fingers into the earth. On the other side of the camp the South Africans were singing their Oompa Loompa songs. I crawled away from them and kept rubbing my head on the ground, combing my hair with the grass. When I was far enough gone from everyone I rolled onto my back, my body in the shape of the cross, like a child pretending to be dead. The trees around me were alive with insect-creaking and the night-prickling stars pinned me down. Things crawled over me, a caterpillar can-can, a millipede march. I felt like Gulliver waking in Lilliput. Somehow I made a connection between the universe and the insects, like the stars were chirping through them - and as is often the case when I am stoned, I made the misapprehension that there was a secret code in all this, a message written out in the world that only I could comprehend.

I must have slept because I woke to hear the sound of a car engine and the South African voices much louder. Picking grass or grubs from my cheek, I Looked at the old Matatu Minibus that the men sometimes used to take tourists from Eldoret to the camp. It drove a little way from the other vehicles and stopped near the camp bins. The South Africans followed and then stood around the edge of the car's light rubbing their hands as if warming them.

I got up and followed them. The car's headlights dipped and illuminated a fan shaped scrub of the ground giving the impression that something illegal was going to happen, that two bare knuckle boxers might step out of the shadows and start to fight. Instead Django sauntered into the light with what looked like a prayer mat and a small bucket. He laid the mat on the ground, ten metres or so in front of the car. For a moment I thought he was going to pray, but he sat cross legged, placing the bucket by his side. The South Africans were totally silent now and I saw Amos stalk around the outside of the circle, a machete in one hand and bucket in the other. He seemed to be throwing things from the bucket out into the night. After a few minutes Django started wailing a name, as if he was calling something long lost out of the darkness. I edged closer to the Matatu. No one noticed me; they were too busy straining to see whatever was out there. Django continued shouting and whistling until the headlights picked out dirty spotted animals padding in and out of the darkness.

Django whistled and kept repeating one Swahili word. From the darkness came a hysterical twittering laugh, more like a bird than a mammal. He draped a slab of meat from the bucket over a small stick and held it out to one side. Sniffing the air, a hyena edged towards him making craven whimpering noises. Suddenly the hyena rushed three paces its jaws snapping at the meat. Then it slunk away and Django whistled again and called another name. In turns the hyenas came, growing in confidence until four of five stood in the car light at one time.

The South African Rastas had their cameras out and were taking photos as close as they dared, but you could see they were afraid to spend too long looking through a camera, unaware of what was behind them. Now Django put the stick in his mouth so the hyenas came jerking their hairy maws right next to his face. As they went for the meat he shifted the stick with a slick move so their salivating teeth clamped down on nothing. All the time he whistled, consoled, decided whose turn it was next. The South Africans were transfixed; one crouched down with his back to the scene, thumbs up and smiling, ready to spring away the moment the picture was taken. At least ten hyenas crept in and out of the light, their small stumpy legs and chunky heads making them look a little like those weedy lions you see on European coats of arms, painted by artists that didn't know any different. They moved with a sort of pregnant gait, their eyes and ears twitching. But with those teeth and jaws they could have crunched through every bone in Django's body.

Eventually he stood up with a shout and the hyenas skulked off. The tourists showed each other their snaps. One put his hand on Django's shoulder to let him see one particular shot. Django nodded, smiling patiently. After a bit he took off his baseball cap.

"Excuse me, please, money for the meat."

The South Africans shuffled and pretended to rummage deep in pockets. A couple of crumpled notes were dropped in the hat, whilst others tried to work out if the note they offered was of low enough value. Django nodded at Amos, who was sitting in the Matatu. The headlight died and we all squinted, trying to make out which shapes in the darkness floated and which shapes walked.

"The meat in this country is not so cheap," said Django waving his machete like a conductor's baton. "And all men can become meat in a moment."

More notes were quickly produced and he pointedly thanked each tourist in turn. When he had been round them all the headlights came back on; the dark shapes disappeared and the hyenas were nowhere to be seen. But we all knew that they were out there watching, baring their teeth, waiting their time.

Chapter Five

I was up at 5.30, fumbling my legs into shorts that still had pants in them, putting on my hoody back to front, failing to find a matching pair of socks. I met Moses and Alfred at the football goal and we did our stretches. Two American steeplechasers who had arrived the previous night joined us, offering moisturised handshakes and toothpaste advert smiles. They seemed immediately at ease making jokes about the hour and talking loudly about their Lariam-affected dreams. Their names were Forrest and Zak; happy and wholesome. I knew that Kirsten would hate them.

It was still half-dark but the farm animals were announcing the start of day with a joyful alarm that suggested they had feared they would never see the sun again. As we trotted down the track to the Kitale Road a preacher with a crackly PA system chastised the countryside from a brightly painted church. Forrest and Zak looked at each other and laughed as the priest worked himself into a greater fury, and the speaker crackled like a plaster being unstuck. Farmers walking to work exchanged Jambos, resigned exhaustion etched into their faces. I always felt guilty bounding along, going places, while they tilled the same muddy clay, or dug holes for fence poles, or chased errant livestock.

My iliotibial bands remained tight from yesterday's double run and I had a slight pain on my outer right knee. My lower abdominal muscles were knotty and I promised myself that I would lay off the circuit sessions for a couple of days. Today we were running 40 minutes at 70% MHR; it was a chance for Alfred to stretch his legs before tomorrow's Cross Country trials. Moses, as was his wont in the morning runs, was wearing a coonskin cap that a girl at his Canadian university had given him and of which he was very proud. He always ended up carrying it for half the run, but it drew curious glances from other runners.

This morning the roads were particularly busy. A shimmer of twenty or so runners, tall and lean like trees that grow too closely together and strain for the sunlight, jogged to the beginning of a loop that they would be timed round. They leaned towards their coach as he issued instructions. Their matching yellow and black vests indicated that they were part of the Fila team.

"Wow!" Zak whooped. "Who are those guys?"

"I'm sure I just saw Eliud Kipchoge," said Forrest.

"Them. They're no-ones," Moses spat dismissively. Alfred smiled shyly, shocked at his daring. Moses put a hand on his friend's shoulder and said, "This is the one you should be looking at. He might not have matching running gear but by tomorrow all Kenya will know him."

Alfred shrugged the hand from his shoulder and ran hard for a few metres, laughing.

"But seriously. Weren't they famous runners? They looked the business."

"They're good runners for sure, but there are hundreds like them. You won't have heard of any of them."

The next group that passed was horribly dressed in frayed, cut up denims, American basketball tops bearing the names of long retired players, and trainers abandoned by the West. They were all quite young but ran with the same steely pride as the Fila team.

The Americans made no comment. It was their first run at altitude and I could see in their stricken glances that the thin air was getting to them. As we looped round by the rail track we had enough elevation to see three other groups of sleek, glossy athletes dreaming along the dirt roads that fanned out of Eldoret. Towards the end of the run a line of girls doing a train session, in which the person at the back of the line has to sprint to the front, creating a new back marker who in turn had to sprint, padded towards us. The Americans cried out "Jambo!" and a couple of them nodded. There was nothing heroic about their faces, just a grim, stoic determination.

As we trailed down to the Ks' farm and Training Centre we passed three big farmsteads with patios and stone walls but no roofs nor any glass in any windows. The street of broken dreams Moses called it – the ranches were all owned by former athletes who had made a lot of money in the first years of their careers and then been hit by injury or lost their hunger and the funds to complete such buildings.

When we got back the orphans were out on the road trying to stop the Christian Cow from making a dash for freedom. The animal sauntered across the driveway, ignoring us. For it the nearest scrub of grass was far more interesting than these white runners everyone seemed to find so ridiculously amusing. The Americans took in the place they were going to call home while doing their warm-down.

"Is that their pet?"

"That's Christmas dinner," I said out of the side of my mouth for fear the cow might hear me.

"Say, isn't this just a training camp?" Forrest suggested.

"I think it started off as a farm. Then they built that quarter to house the kids. As you can see they're still working on the accommodation for the High Altitude Centre. Where we're staying is finished though."

Alfred beckoned me to step away from the Americans and in his soft voice said, "Michael, you remember what we talked about last week, do you?" I nodded uncertainly. "And, it is ok, you will still patronise me?"

Patronise: the word threw me but then I remembered. "Oh my trainers. You can have them in a few days time. I haven't cleaned them yet."

"But tomorrow is the big race."

"I can't get them cleaned and dried by then." He looked at me as if I was making a joke. "In any case, how do you know they'll fit?"

"They'll fit, I'll make them."

"Well ok, here you are. But I warn you, they smell terrible."

He cradled them and, embarrassed, I concentrated on taking my pulse.

"Wow, 82 BPM. That's down from 154 in just three minutes."

The Americans nodded to show they understood the significance of this.

"So how long you been here?" Zak asked.

"Three months."

"Wow, so you're a veteran."

"I guess so," I replied.

"And what other athletes are here?"

"Well, there's Kirsten who I'm with; two Kenyan girls, who medaled at the World junior championship last summer; Alfred and a couple of the farm workers are pretty handy as well. Once they've finished that wing another six junior Kenyan runners should be here."

"Sounds great."

"An opportunity."

"A privilege."

"An honour."

The Americans stretched their hamstrings, batting enthusiasm off each other.

After showering and logging what I had done and how I felt, I ate nine pieces of toast smothered with honey, and two over-ripe bananas. I hung about the dining area waiting for the Americans but they must have gone back to bed. I hadn't weighed myself for three days so did that, then wrote up some of my results. I had dropped to under 60 kilos, which was potentially alarming. Every night I woke two or three times wanting food but unless I had some stored from the shops I went hungry. Kirsten refused to go on the scales, even when I told her it was for my dissertation. She had clearly lost even more weight than me. When she ran with a vest on you could actually make out the shape of her humerus, radius and ulna bones. There were questions I should have asked about her menstrual cycle, and whether she was vomiting or hoarding food, but there was no way I was going to bring up these subjects, not when it was just the two of us training and travelling alone.

I flicked through my spine-broken and book marked copy of *The Complete Anatomy of Stretching* until it was time for my finger stick test. My red blood cell count was increasing at the rate I'd predicted, which was reassuring but uninteresting. It was a shame the Americans had come just as I was leaving, as I would have liked someone else to experiment on. Kirsten's vegetarianism made her an interesting subject but she was less than receptive to the idea of me sticking needles in her.

With nothing to do and no-one to talk to I found myself round at the end of the Training Centre that was still being built. Alfred was there but, as usual when I saw him working, he acted as if he didn't know me.

"Jambo," a man with no front teeth, who occasionally ran with us, hailed from high up on the wooden beams of the half constructed roof. "Come," he shouted waving his hand. I smiled an apology but more of the workers slung themselves round wooden boards, welcoming me to the roof. I started climbing a ladder constructed from two long branches and lots of shorter ones. It looked the sort of structure that the word rickety was coined for, but the only thing shaking was me.

The roof had a few more beams to be added, and the ten or so workers, the ones Kirsten called the Iron Men, were hauling the last remaining lengths of wood into place. A muscular lad called Henry the Carpenter greeted me with a solemn "Hujambo?"

"Sijambo," I replied.

"Nzuri." He smiled, relieved that I had managed to remember this one bit of Kiswahili. Henry had been trying to teach me the language from the first day we arrived. I was ashamed of my total failure to remember even the simplest of expressions and increasingly had avoided working with the men. Of course the fact they could till the clod heavy earth all morning, build a roof in the afternoon and finish the day beating fence posts into the ground, might have contributed to my disinclination to spend time with them. Even with Kirsten to impress I could only work at their rate for half an hour before, palms bleeding and hands cramped in fists, I would admit defeat.

So what I was doing on a roof – dizzy with vertigo and exhaustion, semi-starved and full of anti-malarial drugs that made the world fray and frazzle at the edges – when there was no Kirsten around, was a mystery even to me. Henry indicated that I was to help him lever a large plank into place. Shaking again, the soles of my feet soaked in damp sweat, I edged along one of the fitted boards.

"Look at these weak Kalenjins." Henry waved at two of the other Iron Men. "They are good for running but nothing else."

We managed to haul the rough length of timber into place and Henry nailed it onto the A frame.

"So you're from a different tribe?" I asked once the hammering had finished.

Henry flexed his biceps and the runner with no front teeth wolf whistled. "Do I look like one of these skinny Kalenjins? I am of the Luo. Odaiga, who will be this country's next president, is of my tribe. Do you really not see the difference?"

Looking at him I said, "Now you mention it I do," but I wasn't really sure.

"By the way," the runner with no front teeth said, "they may be strong but they can't run like us."

"Oh, this is a shameless person!" Henry laughed. "Don't believe his untruths."

"What is more, they are always spoiling the air." The runner said sniffing the air and screwing up his nose. One of the others slapped him on the back and Henry started hammering a nail into the piece of timber.

"So, are all the best runners Kalenjins?" I asked the man with no front teeth.

"Almost all."

"Then there must be a genetic rather than an environmental reason for their dominance in distant events."

The man nodded uncertainly and scratched his elbow.

"Put simply," Henry said, "they are nothing but descendents of cattle thieves that have been given spikes and put on a track. You have to be fast to steal cattle."

The Iron Men's attention was taken by the shouts of those on the ground who were carrying a new wooden beam. Everyone got in position and we lifted it up into the roof frame. I had another dizzy moment as I looked down, and had to lean against one of the fitted beams. The wooden frame around me seemed to palpitate and the earth to swell and roll. I was at least five metres off the ground and if I fell was definitely going to break something. The stupidity of the situation was that the cost of medivaccing me out of this place would probably pay a monthly salary to a dozen extra Kenyan workers, men who weren't afraid of heights or worried about getting splinters in their hands, who weren't made dizzy by hard work at altitude and who didn't hallucinate from all the medicines they were taking to help them stay safe in this part of the world.

"A good job is half done." I heard Henry declaring. "Now let us see if that Agnes has prepared some ugali for us."

The men on the roof skipped down the wooden ladder and, trembling down one rung at a time, I followed. Agnes appeared from the kitchen. Seeing the men squatting on the ground she said, "Regular work tires a woman, but destroys a man." Henry chuckled but none of the men dared disagree with her.

Going to pick up the packet of biscuits I'd bought for them provided me with the perfect opportunity to bring my own mug and so avoid borrowing one of the rim-chewed plastic cups that the men shared. Henry the Carpenter was in charge of a big container, the sort you'd use to carry water from a communal tap on camping holidays. In this container was the sweetened diluted ugali. They nibbled the biscuits like children savouring a treat whilst talking about the work they had done and the work that still needed to be completed. There was a feeling of unity amongst them.

Moses came out to see if I was ready for my round of golf. There was only one course, next to a complex called The Central Lounge that had once been a Whites Only type club. The Kenyan political class, the doctors and sons of famous runners, all congregated there, keen to remind you with a mixture of pride and anger that this privilege had once been the exclusive preserve of Europeans. Around the whole area immaculately dressed and pressed security guards stood stiffly behind rolls of razor wire.

I was playing with a priest named Father O'Grady who was head of St Andrew's school, famous for the number of world class runners it had produced. Pot bellied and softly spoken, Father O'Grady looked nothing like a world class sports coach, but over the last 25 years he had trained dozens of athletes who had gone on to become Olympic medallists and World Record holders. I was always trying to find out how he had done this, but it looked like it genuinely pained him to talk about running. Hard work and hunger were about as deep as he went. This would be my last chance to pick his brains, to gather whatever tips he deigned to pass my way.

"You can't play on the club course wearing that. Have you not got something smarter?" said Moses

"Like a Pringle jumper and plus fours?" I joked.

"Exactly." I shook my head. "Well you can borrow some of my clothes, they'll be tight but it's better than shorts and a T-shirt."

For someone who never played golf, Moses had a surprising collection of golfing attire. I got togged out in an Argyll V-neck with a red and yellow diamond pattern, checked trousers that were too short for me, and a white polo neck.

"Am I not going to feel a bit warm or even silly in all this?"

"Don't worry about that. Visor or cap?"

"Er, neither."

"Just make sure you've got socks that match those trousers. "You're showing a bit of ankle."

We loaded the golf bag in the boot and got in the front seats. "What are you doing today?"

"I'm picking my dad up from the airport. I'll meet you at the club at say, five. Then we've got the beauty pageant." He clapped his hands in glee. "We know how to show our guests a good time."

"Is your dad staying long? Please thank him for lending me his clubs. And of course for letting us stay here the last few months."

"You might get to thank him yourself. He'll probably be happier speaking to you than he is to any of us. My brother Gideon, who you'll meet at the trials tomorrow, hasn't spoken to him for three years, all because he does pace making at so many events instead of racing them himself. And he's always rowing with me and Joyce about our grades. But he's set up this orphanage and training camp here, the school in the town. He's one of the fathers of the country. Of course, he's never actually in the country – always off at IAAF meetings or charity dinners in America. You've seen the photos in the sitting room. That's his thing."

Moses gunned the car along the road, scowling at the scabby cattle. He regained some of his cool as we rolled up the beautifully smooth driveway that led to The Central Lounge. A huddle of women fanning fires on which they cooked corn on the cob looked at us more in hope than expectation. The guards, all of whom stood at well over six foot tall, drew themselves to attention in recognition of the car, then slouched when they saw it was only Moses driving. We crunched over the gravel car park filled with polished family cars.

"There are a lot more guards than usual," Moses said as I unloaded my bag.

Next to the Central Lounge was a small club-house where I changed into golfing shoes and waited. Inside, the walls were covered with notices about etiquette and wooden boards naming past club captains and course records. I'd never played golf in my life and had only got roped into this after being grilled by two Kenyan dignitaries who thought living in Scotland qualified me as an expert. Having already disappointed them with my lack of insight into the best whiskies to buy I'd bluffed my way through talk of putters and pars and players I'd never heard of. So it was clear that I was about to make a great fool of myself: for two hours conversation with one of the greatest coaches on the planet this seemed a small price.

Father O'Grady arrived and we walked out to the place where you hit your first shot. "I've not played for a few years," I warned him, "and what's more, I'm left handed and these clubs are for a right handed player."

The first hole seemed to be incredibly long but I hacked myself onto the green in four hits and put the ball in the hole after two more.

"Are you going to the Cross Country tomorrow?" I asked. He didn't answer until he had played a drive that curled into a sandy hole on the second.

"Of course not," he said looking shocked. "I've mass to take."

On the green I continued my inquiries. "Are there any of your athletes I should look out for?"

"Well, most of them have the potential to make the national team, but it's a hard one to call. You'll see for yourself. There're always a few total unknowns that don't run for a team but make an impact at the front of the field, especially at junior level. This year I'm more excited about our middle distance runners. I've got a fantastic group of 17, 18 year olds who'll do great things this summer."

"I'm a middle distance runner as well, although my coach likes me to do cross countries in the winter."

"It's a good thing."

I took a swipe which went very high and landed about 40 metres in front of me. "This right-handed thing really isn't easy."

"You'd get along better if you weren't using a pitch and wedge to drive."

"These middle distance prospects, what sort of times will they be doing?"

"Well, there's one lad, David, who I'm sure will run 1:43 for the 800 this season. A lot of people think he's got the potential to break Wilson's great record."

"Jesus. That's pretty fast." We zigzagged our way to the third green. "I've done 1:50 for the 800 and 3:44 for the 15."

"What age are you supposed to be?"

"Twenty next week."

"Are you studying?"

"I'm in the third year of a Sports Science degree. They funded me to come out here and do research."

"Well, stick at it."

"And the times?"

"Not bad."

"Not bad for a British junior, but out here I wouldn't be noticed. The men at the Ks' farm said that all the best runners are Kalenjins. Is that true, are they just naturally better than us?"

Father O'Grady scowled, concentrating on a long putt that skittered around the hole.

"Well for starters, not all the best runners are Kalenjins, and when they compete whether they are Kalenjin, Kikuyu or Luo does not matter, they are representing Kenya. But yes, it's one factor. Wilson Kipketer, whose 800 metre World Record has lasted a decade, ran only the fourth fastest time in the list of our school's best runners. So there are plenty of people with talent to burn. Of course living and training at altitude plays a big part, as it does for the best Ethiopian and Moroccan runners. But the most important thing is the training camp.

"Iten, where we're based, has about 4000 people and half of them run. They come there because we have the best training groups. Some live six, seven to a room, get up every morning before sunrise to latch on to one of the groups in the hope that someone will see their potential and ask them to join. Then when they're in the group they train three times a day. Run, eat, sleep, repeat. That's all they do; there's no secret. Even if they're married with children they will only see their family once or twice a month. For entertainment they watch old videos of races. This fuels them as much as the food we supply. They run on dreams. It's the only thing most of them have. Look around you at the slums in Eldoret. Of course their dreams are going to be more precious to them than yours are to you."

I'd heard most of what he was saying before and could accept him telling me what was real, but not him telling me what I could dream. Kirsten's dad had a five year plan for me that involved peaking for the next Olympic Games. In my mind there was no doubt I would be there. I drove first on the next hole, channelling my frustrations into hitting the ball really far. I sliced it spectacularly into some trees.

"Are you sure you've played this game before?"

"Not really."

"And you're not actually left-handed, are you?"

"Nope."

He chuckled. "You're actually pretty good for a beginner." He took out a driver and hit his ball plumb down the middle of the fairway. "Let's not talk about running any more, it's all people ever speak to me about. I want to hear news from home: who's going to win the Premiership, is Scotland going to become independent, what films and books are people talking about."

So we went round the rest of the course, and I talked and he listened, occasionally mumbling admonishments as if the problems of the country were my fault, before gently encouraging me to go on and confess all of our sins.

Back at The Central Lounge he said, "Britain is fat and decadent now. Its glory days are over. How can a country which hands instant fame, money and celebrity to glorified karaoke singers or someone living in a house full of cameras expect its people to become good at something that requires hard work? I mean real blood, sweat and tears, hard work, something that demands thousands of hours of effort every year. How can they even know what this is?" He mopped his brow with a stained handkerchief that had started the day crisp and white.

I accepted his assessment even though it was no different from the sort of thing people had been telling me for years. In any case I was going to prove him wrong. His pessimism just strengthened my resolve. We shook hands and said our goodbyes.

I spotted Kirsten, Joyce and two of her friends sitting round a table on the verandah and went over to say hello. The Kenyan girls were all lip gloss and giggles but Kirsten sat hugging her knees, chewing her lower lip as if it was something to be savoured. Unable to get any sensible conversation out of them I left with my head bowed, affecting a limp, like an athlete who has been spiked and, instead of running on, hirples off the track.

I went to the dining area and, after interrogating the barman over whether they used bottled water to make all their drinks, ordered a mango juice. I loitered there, spying on the group of girls, unsure if I really wanted to join them.

A couple of middle aged women who worked for some NGO or other waved me over, but I pretended to be consulting the menu. In loud moneyed voices one ordered the Lounge's famous spaghetti bolognaise, demanding that the pasta be "al dente, not the usual slop," while the other sought confirmation that the tuna salad contained, "real tuna steak and not some ship floor scrapings out of a can."

They sipped at their G & Ts content that they had made themselves clear. After a few minutes, however, they could restrain themselves no longer and started to bemoan the fact that they weren't working in Nairobi, which at least had a Hilton.

I felt bad just being there. The most luxurious place for 100 km and these people with the same skin as I were ripping it apart. A young couple in perhaps their best clothes sat holding hands across the table trying not to listen. The cost of the food here was many times more than at any of the city restaurants. Perhaps the man had saved for this treat for months to celebrate a birthday or anniversary. I felt doubly bad after what Father O'Grady had told me. What was I doing sitting on this cushioned chair, dressed like some country gent and waiting to be taken to a beauty pageant when I should be back at the High Altitude Centre getting ready for a hard session?

At this moment a waiter in perfectly pressed trousers and a white jacket crossed the floor with their orders, a tight-rope walker's concentration on his face.

"Tuna salad," he announced, a slight tick on his handsome face betraying the fact he feared trouble was in store. "And the spaghetti bolognaise."

"This isn't steak," Tuna Salad gasped.

"No, it's tuna."

"But I specifically," and at this point she scanned the whole bar for witnesses, and everybody pretended to be contending with some particularly taxing mental arithmetic or staring into the eyes of a loved one, "ordered Tuna steak!" She took a deep breath and arched her back. "I'm sorry but I'll have to speak to your manager."

The man shuffled an imaginary Rubik's cube in his hands and after executing half a bow retreated like a drunken uncle doing the moonwalk at a wedding party.

"Have you ever seen the like?" Tuna Salad exclaimed to no one in particular.

In solidarity Spaghetti Bolognaise sat with hands on her lap, the pasta cooling in front of her. After a few minutes the manager walked reluctantly to the table. With his hands behind his back like someone who doesn't want to provoke a fight he asked, "What seems to be the problem?" And at that point Moses and a friend arrived dressed as a pair of hip-hop harlequins.

"Nice threads," the friend said. "My name is Jeremiah, I

study at Cambridge University, hence my English grammar and pronunciation are more or less perfect."

"Yes, they seem to be very good." I stood and offered my hand. Jeremiah gave me a slippery fish sort of handshake. "What is it you're studying?"

"Art history," he chuckled as if the question was irrelevant, "but I'll probably end up in politics. It's the only way anyone makes any real money in this country." After consulting a watch that he kept on a chain in the inside pocket of his perfectly cut velvet jacket he remarked, "Time to shake a leg old chap. You'll want a good view tonight."

"Your sister's outside, she seems to be acting a little weird." Moses snatched the hat from his head and peered onto the verandah, then ducked back.

"She's probably stoned," he said in a disgusted tone.

"You mean drunk?"

"I mean stoned from smoking too much marijuana."

"And Kirsten?"

He shrugged and following Jeremiah's lead put his hat on and headed for the door. Moses was driving, and for some reason Jeremiah sat in the back with me as if we were being chauffeured.

"So what do you think of the apparel?" Jeremiah asked, stretching out his arms so I could admire his jacket and cuffs.

"You look like an African Beau Brummell."

"Fantastic!" Jeremiah beamed. "A man who knows how to pay a compliment. Moses and I are on a mission to try and dandify Africa. It will not be easy." He waved out the window at the ramshackle huts that looked as though they'd been struck by some natural disaster. "This I bought on Saville Row." He flicked the jacket open to show me the label. "Naturally my shoes are Italian."

I wasn't sure if this was meant to be some grand pastiche of past colonialists or simply an attempt to ape the European elite so, I replied, "Naturally." Moses kept glancing at me in the mirror, trying to see how far I would go along with this subversion.

"I have an original Jaguar coupé at home. The only one of its kind in Eastern Africa. What a shame we can't take it out tonight but there is something the matter with the engine and the parts have to be shipped from Britain." He laughed like a person unable to believe his own excesses. "Your father's friend, Kip Keino, must be so proud that they are holding a beauty contest in the stadium they named after him," Jeremiah mocked. "May I ask your opinion of Kenyan girls?"

"Well," I struggled, relieved that the dying light concealed my blushes, "like girls everywhere, some are very beautiful, some are not."

"You will make a great diplomat. Personally I am indifferent to girls and Kenyan ones in particular. Moses however tells me you brought a fine example of an English girl with you."

"I didn't say that," Moses started but Jeremiah silenced him with a raised finger.

"Shit," Moses cursed, slamming on the brakes.

"Oh, this is sad." Jeremiah frowned at a line of truck tyres that had been dragged across the street to form a blockade.

"Should I try and turn?"

"No, we shall proceed in a calm manner."

Moses slung his hat on the passenger's seat, untied his cravat and edged the car forward. A group of about fifteen young men huddled round the car in front of us, interrogating the driver. As they turned into our headlights I saw they were carrying machetes, hammers and cleavers.

Moses cracked his window open a couple of inches and one of the men shone his torch at our faces. Others surrounded the car gently rocking it with their hands. "Kalenjins?"

"All Kalenjins," Moses replied, which in my case was clearly a lie.

"No Kikuyu or Luo?"

"No."

"You. What are your names?" They asked Jeremiah whose voice and body shook as he answered. After flicking the torch light on my face they spoke to Moses in a fast and harsh language that I couldn't understand.

"It is too dangerous to go on," he translated. "There's been a political rally and it's turned nasty."

Suddenly someone started chattering and my door was opened. Hands tugged at me, shiny black faces with bulging crazed eyes excited by some new game glared at me.

"Camera," one shouted. "Camera make photo."

I climbed out of the car and lifted the camera. They backed away from me as if it was a gun.

"Wait!"

Another snatched Jeremiah's Trilby. There was laughter as two of the men fought over the hat. They crowded together making hip hop poses and brandishing their weapons, their baggy clothes concealing scrawny bodies, their defiant sneers hiding any fear. "Again, again," they shouted clambering on the tyres and shouting threats at the night.

"Let me see," the man with the torch said. "Yes, yes. This is good." The others crowded round laughing at their bravado. "We're unburogable!" They shouted. I didn't know what this meant but was sure I agreed. The man with the torch went into a pocket and pulled out a scrap of paper. Draping an arm over my shoulder he lent into me like an injured friend, filling my nostrils with his compost stink. "This is my address and these my digits. You send me these photos by email or else." One gave me a pretend cuff on the back of the head and I stumbled back towards the car. The gang cackled, keen to see how I would react, then made strange sexualised gestures as Moses led me back to the car. Jeremiah must have locked the doors and we had to bang on the window until he opened. I jumped into the leather-smelling air conditioned safety of the back seat and slammed the door shut. As Moses u-turned hands drummed on the boot of the car and there was a great cheer as we drove off.

No one said anything for a couple of minutes.

"When I started at Cambridge I had this notion from reading your fashion and celebrity magazines. I thought it would be a great idea to make one of these but using photos of the poor and destitute of this country juxtaposed with bitchy comments about fashion triumphs and faux pas. We would do features on certain totally normal local characters as if they were famous, as if they were people anyone cared about. Dieting tips turned on their head, giving advice on how to fatten up your children or husband when you haven't enough money. Horoscopes that predicted how many times you'd be robbed or raped or ripped off this month – all in that cheery know-it-all style. But I came to realise it would never work. My country is not ready for irony and your country is not ready for the truth."

A van with eight policemen sitting upright in the back, berets on their head, dark waterproofs over their shirts caused Moses to veer off the road. Jeremiah watched them pass; his jaw muscles clenched, and his eyes were wet. "Now all I hope is that they shoot them all."

We cruised the streets for a few minutes with Moses and Jeremiah trying to contact people on their mobiles to see what was up. No one was answering and I hoped Moses would give up and go home. There were no streetlights anywhere near the Ks' but I would still have plenty of time for an exercise circuit before bed. Finally he got through to someone and after a short conversation said, "Joyce and her friends are out on Oginga Odinga Street."

Jeremiah screwed up his face as if the news left a bitter taste. "Have you been there at night?"

I shook my head.

"My mother says it is the modern day Sodom and Gomorrah." Moses laughed.

"It is not as good as that," Jeremiah objected. "For that you'd have to visit Nairobi or Mombasa."

"We're going to both of those cities next week."

"Well if I were you, I would pay a visit to the Paradise Nightclub in Mombasa. A very fine establishment. Certainly superior to anything on Oginga Odinga Street."

"But you can find anything you want on Oginga Odinga Street, just keep your eyes open and your wits about you."

We swung into a squabble of taxis as a Matatu shuddered past us, painted cherry red and with the Ferrari logo crudely emblazoned on the sliding door. Moses nudged the car into a space. We parked next to a vehicle whose operators were crying prices and routes to partygoers, many of whom didn't seem put off by the slogan *Drive with the best and die like the rest* graffitied on the van's side.

The air was thick with heavy stabs of bass lines from various clubs. We got out of the car and Moses and Jeremiah strode down the pavement, clearly feeling powerful in their elegant clothes. I tried to feel as confident in my skin-tight golfing attire. Street hawkers offered cups of steaming tea which Moses rejected and boiled eggs and roasted hazelnuts which Jeremiah said would fuel me if I was hoping to make any sexual conquests.

We turned into a dark doorway, stretched in front of which was a carpet that must once have been red but now was the colour of a sickly tongue. The bouncers ushered us in before a crowd of others. Before we were lost in the club's darkness Moses warned me, "If a man asks you to meet his sister, the chances are that the girl is not really his sister."

Moses and Jeremiah seemed to know everyone in the club, and we struggled through many shifty and complicated handshakes before arriving at the bar. I bought a coke for myself and beers for the boys. The place was so dark that it was hard to make out the size of note I was pulling from my wallet. Moses spotted his sister and headed over to dance. The whole place was going off in a way that only seems to happen in every single rap video ever made: about 80% of the people dancing were girls in tiny shorts and bikini tops, while guys in their baggies made no pretence of concealing that they were checking them out. Everyone danced like a choreographer had been working on them for weeks. The thought of joining in horrified and excited me.

The taller of Joyce's friends slinked across the dance floor. She was wearing gold hot pants and red lacquered high heels. I couldn't keep my eyes off her fat black thighs. She was walking right towards me, monstrously sexy with the extra elevation.

"Dancing?" She asked.

"Later," I replied, meaning *not in a million years but Christ I'd like to if I weren't such a stiff-limbed coward.* She pulled an exaggerated sulk and sauntered back to the dance floor.

"I am not someone who likes to lose himself in festivities either," Jeremiah confided. "I prefer to watch."

We leant against the bar and I saw Kirsten in the middle of the writhing crowd looking totally out of place in a running T-shirt and tight black jeans. Around her a group of grinding hip-hop boys, shirts unbuttoned and caps askew, looked at her. I pulled out another of my resealable plastic bags in which I carried a number of straws. While these were not sterile they had to be better than drinking from some recycled bottle that half the city had slobbered on.

Jeremiah watched as I sipped on the straw. "Splendid," was all he said

We drank and contemplated and peeled the labels from our respective bottles, dropping them on the floor.

"You want to keep an eye on your girlfriend," Jeremiah warned. I felt the music vibrating through the floor, shaking my legs, the bass drum thumping deep in my diaphragm as I thought of being surrounded by those painted smiles and earthy smells. "No, really, you should get out there. That girl dancing with Moses is a decoy."

"What do you mean?"

"I mean the people around them are thieves."

I excused my way across the dance floor but, sober and stiff, found it impossible to sway through the crowds. A stunning girl in a sparkly boob tube halted me with a pursing of her lips and started dancing up against me saying words I would never hear. Jeremiah pushed me on and just as we got near our friends a commotion broke out. Moses seemed to be fighting with a man, then another pushed him to the floor. Kirsten stood with her hands covering her face like a cartoon of someone in shock. I rushed over to her, unsure if she was laughing or crying.

"They've taken my bag," was all she said.

There seemed to be a rush for the door and I followed, thinking I could see Kirsten's suede satchel. Bustling out onto the street, I wrestled through the smell of diesel engines and hazelnuts, the tangle of passing people. I followed three men but they could have been anyone really. They went into a 24 hour chemist's and I realised they weren't carrying the bag. I walked back to the club, but the black painted doors were shut and the bouncers nowhere to be seen. Already bystanders were pausing as they passed, poking their heads out of Minibuses. I felt a wave of panic, sure that all these people were looking at me, waiting for me to do something. Banging on the door, I shouted, "Let me in!" but the music was still pounding and there was no response. A Matatu ticket seller for no particular reason started banging on the door with me, yelling in Kiswahili. One moment my noisy ally was there, the next he was thrust away and a giant of a policeman, with a stave taller than he was, tapped on my shoulder. Another policeman was striking the legs of the Matatu ticket seller who jigged back to his vehicle. The giant policeman gave the door a smart rap with his knuckles and a bouncer opened up. Kirsten burst out. I tried to take her in my arms but she stood looking at the street as if she never knew such a place existed.

"Are you all right?" She peered around her with big baby blinks like someone coming out of a cave.

"My camera, that bag had my camera in it."

"She's all right," I told a chubby officer, whose white gloves and square head gave him an air of authority. He said something to me in Kiswahili and I replied with a thumbs-up and slowly, loudly, like some half-witted tourist repeated, "All right."

Joyce came out and gave Kirsten's arm a squeeze. "Man, why did that have to happen? I was dancing with a really hot guy."

Moses was talking to the police, taking control of the situation, while Jeremiah leant back against a corrugated iron wall smoking a black tipped cigarette. He seemed to be deriving intense satisfaction from the situation. The police and bouncers brought five men from the club and lined them up. Like a wall of football players before a particularly ferocious free kick they stood twitching, wondering which parts of their body to protect. The square-headed policeman walked towards them. He was the only one not carrying a stave but the sight of him made them flinch.

"They closed the club doors to trap the thief inside." Moses told Kirsten. "Please don't worry, they will apprehend the criminal."

The little man was shouting into the face of the first suspect phlegm flailing from his lips. The man stood looking at the end of his old but well polished brown brogues shaking his head.

"They've got the wrong people," Kirsten said.

Moses relayed the message to the investigating officer and after a small argument said, "They know these people. They are the right ones. Even if they didn't commit this crime they are guilty of something."

The man at the end of the line tried to slink off but two tall policemen set about him, cracking his shins with their sticks. Once he had gone to ground they slapped him a few times in the face and dragged him across the street to their headquarters.

"This is too heavy," Kirsten whispered, "I never wanted this to happen." She looked frightened and I'd never seen her that way before. It made me feel powerful. I wanted to lecture her on her behaviour since we'd been here, tell her how this was the outcome of her over-friendliness, her naive belief that everyone was essentially good.

The square-headed officer took out a notebook. "May I have the young lady's name and address?"

Kirsten drew back appalled, as if what he was asking was unreasonable.

"Her name's Kirsten Harrison. She's an athlete, staying at the Ks' training centre," I added, hoping that reference to our famous host would have its usual impact

"Mr K." The man nodded as if this was what he had expected. "Interesting."

He went back to interrogating the line of frightened men.

"Don't you like Kenyan justice?" Jeremiah scoffed. "So efficient, so effective!" Kirsten looked at him doubtfully. Like me she was finding it difficult to understand whether every word he said was meant sarcastically. "By the way, what did you have in your handbag?"

"A camera . . . it had something important on it."

"Your little snippets of Africa. The evidence that you've been, seen, conquered. Anything else?"

"Some cosmetics, a few packets of chewing gum, about 3000 shillings, nothing important really."

"3000 shillings." Jeremiah tutted. "Down this lane, there are prostitutes that sell their bodies for twenty."

"Twenty!"

"They are very disappointing prostitutes, old and not even pleasant to look at."

"But twenty shillings, I bought a packet of tissues for that."

"Yes, but you can't wipe your nose on a prostitute," Jeremiah replied thoughtfully.

A vast crowd now encircled the dirty red carpet at the entrance to the club and, with the garish flashing lights, cacophony of music and line of suspects, I felt part of some great and horrible pantomime.

"Come, come," the interrogator bade Kirsten. "Now you will make identification."

Kirsten shrank back and had to be led hunch-shouldered

to stand in front of the men. Each made passport photo faces trying to mask surges of fear, guilt or desperation.

"I've never seen any of these men before."

"Excuse me, but you will tell us."

"She doesn't recognise them," I remonstrated.

The square headed interrogator eyeballed us for a minute. "You are not making a fabrication so that you can claim money on insurance?"

"No."

"Then you will make identification."

"Come on Kirsten."

"I can't."

"You must." She shook her head, looking at the suspects' shoes. "Maybe tomorrow, she's in shock."

"It doesn't matter," the interrogator said, "we know who is the guilty one here."

There was a rumble of voices from the crowd as the suspects were led across the street, policemen striking at the legs of those who got in their way. The faces surrounding us didn't even try to conceal their hatred.

"What am I doing here? What are we doing here?" Kirsten mumbled. "We should never have come." The bulging eyes, hands tugging at my sleeve, the hypnotic thud of music all fell away and for a moment we could have been standing anywhere. "I want to go home," she whispered, as though it was a long held secret finally confessed.

I nodded like I'd known this all along. "Don't worry. I'm taking you there."

Chapter Six

I woke with that furry tongue in my fat head and sorrow, just sorrow in my heart. I couldn't even remember the faces of those poor men lined up in front of me. But their shoes, their well worn, well loved shoes: I'd never forget them. I was always full of bitter self-hatred after a smoking session but this was the worst I'd ever felt. As I shuffled into the bathroom to clean my teeth the full extent of the horror hit home. Not only were some blameless men locked up because of me, but my camera was lost, or even worse, in the hands of police. What would they do if they looked at my film of the protest? We were leaving Eldoret in 13 hours; in that time anything could happen. But what was the worst they could do? Lock me up, beat me. Not for the first time, I wished my conscience was as easy to clean as my teeth.

It wasn't light yet but sleep was out of the question. I decided to go for a run. Once after a session Alfred had said that he had run so hard he had forgotten his own name. That was the sort of oblivion I wanted.

So I did my stretches, put on my trainers, and went out into the dregs of the night. The farm dogs howled but it wasn't them I feared. The blackness was being washed out of the sky and I knew I deserved whatever I got. My lungs felt clogged up with smoke and I had a wretched taste in my mouth. Soon though I had run this off and was feeling better, lighter, more clear-headed. Running is a question mark hanging over each day: If I don't run I feel uneasy, and I can't get my untired body to sleep, and when it does I have dreams in which I chase things I am never going to catch, or I am chased by something from which I'll never escape, and my laces are untying themselves, and the elastic in my shorts snapping.

As it was Sunday, and so early in the day, I didn't see any of the usual faces. After three months we knew those who would say 'Jambo,' (almost everybody) and those who would not. I always looked for a woman who cycled an old-fashioned bike with terrific poise. She wore a flower print dress and a cagoule, no matter the weather. I thought she was probably a teacher, she had that sort of assurance. She never said 'Jambo' but smiled serenely as though she was listening to beautiful music on hidden headphones.

Twenty minutes passed before I saw the first people, cutting down the newly erected telephone polls that Moses said they would burn to make charcoal. Seeing me, they dropped their axes on the ground and struck poses like people trying to solve complex philosophical problems. I picked up the pace. My legs felt fresh after two days rest and I ran further along that road than ever before, putting in bursts of pace, a minute off, a minute on. I pushed myself hard because I wanted to hurt. Running was the cleanest and best way I knew to punish myself. For runners like Mike it's different. They are fuelled by self-love, a need to improve themselves, to wallow in their superiority.

After picking a spot at the top of a small slope I jogged raggedly up the gradient, recovering my breath. I was so wrapped up in my thoughts that I didn't hear the sound of someone gasping behind me.

Mike's face burst into my meditative morning. Even in the early cool, it was slick with sweat. I slowed to allow him to join me. He took about 20 seconds to catch his breath and said, "Why did you leave so early? We could have run together."

I shrugged. One of the fundamentals of Kenyan running is the training group, and while I can see why this works it really isn't for me. I prefer running alone, lost in that sumptuous solitariness, with my own breath and pulse for company.

We ran back together, talking occasionally about today's trials, about how our legs were feeling, about any unusual effects we were experiencing from training at altitude: the usual things. Mike avoided mentioning last night's episode. The run back seemed much longer than the run out.

When we arrived at the farmstead Gladys was waiting on the veranda.

"Well at least you had the sense to run together. I am so angry with those two. Me, what I know is that Oginga Odinga Street is a wicked place at the best of times so what were they thinking taking you there ten days before an election?" She looked in the direction of the city as if she could see the approach of a marauding army. "Sammy!" she snapped, noticing the boys playing football. "If you get your good trousers dirty I shan't take you to church." Sammy contemplated whether to take this as a threat or an encouragement. "And is that the ball that Kirsten brought from Scotland? You know that is only to be used on special occasions. "

After breakfast we travelled to Iten, home of distance running in Kenya in the heart of Kalenjin country and the venue for today's race. It was strange going to an event as a spectator. Faith sat next to me, playing piano on her knees, screwing and unscrewing the cap of her water bottle without drinking, while one foot tapped out the rhythm of her own nervous energy. Faith, Sylvia and Alfred were the ones condemned to race today. They were silent and fascinating. Even Mike had become respectful towards them and had stopped reading from *The Gigantic Book of Inspirational Quotations*.

We hadn't been invited to compete, it wasn't our race. But you know, on the few occasions I had gone to Cross-Countries in Scotland snug and smug in a warm jacket I had always ended up feeling gridlocked with guilt. Racing round a muddy field in the sleet wearing only a vest and shorts in front of a smattering of long-suffering friends or family members probably seems senseless to you. Certainly there is no glory in it and very little money. So when a race was starting and I argued with myself about whether to remove my hands from the comparative warmth of my pockets and clap, I usually felt glad it wasn't me. But by half way, with the lead runner's legs pink with the cold and splattered with mud, snot hanging from her chin, a haunted look on her sweaty gaunt face, it was just too much for me. I would feel shamed because she was out there and I was standing, stalking her, in comparative comfort; even if I was injured or running in a bigger race the next day it just seemed unfair. She was suffering and I was not and she seemed the lucky one.

So I knew that watching the trials at Iten would be an uncomfortable experience. Moses introduced us to his oldest brother, Gideon, who had been the pace maker for the Ethiopian runner Kenenisa Bekele during many of his World Record breaking attempts. He had a shiny bald head that was so perfectly shaped you wanted to rub your hands round. He was quite beautiful really, one of those pedigree human beings who you can just tell will be fast. Man, with his easy movements and his supernatural grace he could have been from another species.

A gun went off and Gideon solemnly said, "The race has commenced."

We watched as the combined junior and senior women sprinted past us. There were about eighty runners and all of them looked world class. Most had their hair braided or cut short so as not to distract them. They were skeletal; their collar bones looked like ornaments. The cleanliness of colourful vests against black shiny skin was almost too bright to look at. Sylvia and Faith were in the leading group but one girl with only a pair of socks on her feet had gone off hard and was already 20 metres clear of the others. She seemed to be smiling.

"This is so motivating," said Mike bouncing on the spot as if he wanted to chase after them.

"Motivating? Terrifying is more like it."

Gideon nodded, and in the perfect English that all the K children spoke said, "You should see the national cross country trials. Imagine you are me, a senior runner trying to make a living from this sport. You watch the junior's race and there are these kids that no one has even heard of. The race starts and they sprint until they drop. There are hundreds of them."

The leader appeared on the brow of the hill, with a line of stickwomen chasing.

"They'll catch her," predicted Mike. We hopped back into the car and raced along the dirt road to a point where we could see the runners reappear. The quality was such that the field didn't get strung out but bounded along in large packs as if on a training run. Mike got out his camera and took shots of Sylvia and Faith as they passed.

"These are great," he enthused, looking at his photos.

"I'd forgotten you had a camera."

"I'm always unsure about taking photos of people in town. It just seems too much of an intrusion."

"But there're so many great photos to be taken."

"Maybe you're right, but it just feels wrong, like stealing from someone who can't afford it."

"I know what you mean. You see these exhibitions back home, stunning images ripped from places like this. The people in the photos could never have imagined the whitewashed galleries that their faces ended up in."

"Nor could the people admiring the images imagine the poverty in which these people live."

"That's why the images have such power," I exclaimed, sure that we were onto something. "We strain at the photos trying to empathise, while they look back: calm, confused or curious. We don't know what their lives are like but we know how to read expressions and the faces in these photos are so expressive that we feel we know the subject's inner most thoughts. Everyone knows that the Indians believed people lost part of their soul when photographed but maybe it was more that they lost the ability to express emotion on their face. When you compare the beautifully bland film stars and models to people who are hardly ever in front of a camera it sort of makes sense"

Mike was looking at me in an *I'm concerned about your*

ranting but interrupting would be like stopping a sleep walker and so it's best not to get involved sort of way. "So should I take photos or not?"

After thinking for some time I said, "Do whatever feels best."

Gideon spotted some spectators he knew and jumped out of the car so he could speak to them.

"Who is that again?" Mike asked.

I recognised one of the men but couldn't put a name to his face. "Someone famous?"

"I know that."

We drove back to the finish line to watch the runners coming round for the second lap. The girl in socks was still in the lead but she was getting dragged back into the leading pack and was no longer smiling.

I thought they'd all gone off too hard but the pace continued relentlessly. It wasn't until we saw them for the third time that the girl, now wearing only one sock and carrying the other in her hand, had been overtaken and the lead group broken into twos and threes. Faith had fallen far off the pace but Sylvia was on the shoulder of the lead runner, still graceful, still strong. Her cheek bones, thighs, the top of her shoulders, shone as they caught the sunlight. We were so excited by this point that there was no way we were getting back into the jeep to watch the finish. Instead we ran, and what a relief it was. The famous man, who I now realised looked almost exactly like Paul Tergat, bounded past bawling encouragement at the female racers. We reached a vantage point where we could see the leading girl sprint down the red dirt road, her look of concentration breaking into one of glory as she realised she was far enough clear and would make the finish line. She was cheered on by male runners, townspeople and half a dozen men in suits. Sylvia ran in to hold on to second place but looked despondent, knowing she was well beaten.

I jogged over, not knowing whether to console or congratulate her.

"She bested me today," she said, washing sweat and grit from her forehead with water from a bottle, "so in January she will fly." She glugged some water and gasped for air. "But next time I will win her. You mark my words."

I turned to Moses' brother for some explanation and realising I didn't understand he said, "The prize for this race is a paid invitation to a 10 Km in Germany. Once there the athlete has a great opportunity to win some money and maybe get invited to future events."

"Well you're still only eighteen," I squeezed Sylvia's bony shoulder.

She winced and then, trying to smile, said, "There are so many great female road warriors." Glancing at the other runners and speaking as if imparting a great secret she added, "For every hundred of us only one or two will ever fly."

A beat-up bus came hooting down the road and the athletes huddled to the sides. Once it had passed one of the suited men dug his heel into the rutted road so that everyone could make out the finishing line again. The men were doing 50 metre sprints, high knee drills and back kicks. There were a lot more of them competing than in the women's race. Again, all looked like they were warming up for some Golden League meeting in Europe rather than a local trail race.

"How far do the men run?"

"They must surround the big field twice, then over speed to the line," Sylvia sipped from her bottle. "I go over to Faith now. See if she is somehow ok."

Moses' brother chewed his lower lip and said, "This is going to be some competition." He had a stopwatch in one hand which he kept checking even though the runners hadn't started. "What your friend says is true. Only a very few will make any real money from this. If they do make it there is the opportunity to make millions but this is only for the real elite.

"Me, I have made some money but mostly from pace making. My father doesn't like it but if you are a good pace maker you will be well paid and furthermore you know how much you are making before a race. I have a wife and two small children to think of. Before I had them I would always race competitively. Once in a 5000 metres Grand Prix I was at the front of a pack with 200 metres to go. It had been a slow race so there was a sprint for the line. I came in eighth. For that I got $500. The man who won that day, a great friend of mine, finished first and won $15,000. He was less than two seconds in front of me but that two seconds can make or break a man. You have lived out here long enough to know what that type of money can buy, what that type of money can save you from."

The race started, and about two hundred men blazed towards us in elegant, sprightly haste. The sounds of their feet crunching on the dry dirt, their arms beating against the air and the artificial fabrics rustling in the breeze seemed somehow insignificant after the crack of the gun. Their brightly coloured vests and shorts disappeared over the first hill, a smoky red cloud hanging in their wake.

"I don't think I could keep up with them for 200 metres," said Mike, only half joking. Like me I could see that watching others run troubled him. Practically skipping on the spot, he waited for me before we rushed off to a vantage point.

We tried to spot the yellow and blue of Alfred's vest but others were sporting similar colours. "Is that him?" Mike asked.

"I don't know."

"Yeah, I'd forgotten that you couldn't tell the difference between them."

I couldn't decide if this was a dig at my refusal to identify anybody at last night's line up. A runner much taller than the others had opened up a lead but a big group with two yellow and blue vests in it was not far behind him. As they approached us the tall runner turned and gestured as if to encourage some of the others to take on the pace. We recognised Alfred at the back of the group.

When the runners had passed, Mike said, "Do you know Robert Blair?"

"Was he the one that crapped himself at the national relays and kept running?"

"Well yes, but he's also a bloody good athlete and it *was* a relay event." I shrugged and he continued, "When he came back from the World Junior Cross Country a few years back he was really depressed. He'd come 80th or something like that. To cheer him up your dad tried to point out that he was the 80th best junior at something in the whole world – which is pretty amazing. Robert had sort of agreed but then laughed and said if the Kenyans had been allowed another 100 runners in their team instead of 6 he'd probably have been 180th. Now I know what he meant."

Screams of encouragement announced that the runners were coming round for the second lap. Mike raised a fist that I suppose was meant to be holding a make believe microphone to his face. My grandfather who, like my dad, had run for Great Britain, was quite a famous commentator for the BBC in the 1970s. He had a Yorkshire accent that Mike tried to emulate as the runners came into sight.

"And three athletes have now broken clear. The local favourite with the long loping stride, followed by an Iten runner from the Fila team and hot on their heels the green vested underdog, covering the ground effortlessly."

"Sometimes you're just too much," I said, shamed for his attempts to amuse or annoy.

"And here comes Arthur Kipkoech, a little off the pace but sure to show his class as the race develops."

The runners passed, the flowing effortless strides that they had all started with now looking more strained as their arms punched the air and their tight faces grimaced.

"He's certainly not going to win."

"He might be well up amongst the juniors."

Mike again raised the imaginary microphone to his face and adjusted a non-existent ear piece, "And here we have probably the greatest concentration of world class participants in a single sport anywhere in the world. The competition here is fiercer than it is to be a footballer in Brazil, or a boxer in Mexico. If you can win here you can win anywhere. We're just waiting on the leaders coming in, any thoughts on how this race has developed, Kirsten?" He thrust the make believe microphone up to my face so that my lips brushed against his fist and I breathed in that antiseptic smell of his. "No, I didn't think so. But here they come and this is going to be a real carve up, the tall runner with the moustache still leads, but hanging on for dear life is the Fila sponsored athlete, and the green vested underdog isn't out of it yet. They're into the home straight now and the Fila runner makes his move but the tall runner matches him and moves clear, what a race this is! Tall runner, Fila runner, tall runner moves away to win it by a couple of strides. Fantastic stuff."

We jogged down to watch Alfred come in 25th, a look of bitter disappointment seared into his face. He collected his bottle of water, limply shook the hands of other runners, and didn't make eye contact with anyone.

"What am I going to do?" he said as I passed him a towel. "I might as well give up now. There were five other junior runners in front of me. Five. I am so disgusted with myself. This vest was given to me by Mr K!" He pounded his chest. "I am not fit to wear it."

He turned away. I started to go after him with a change of T-shirt before realising that he needed to be by himself. This wasn't going to be easy, as the other runners were now crossing the line in large numbers. Those that had already finished did slow motion pas de basques around the finishing area. After running in a straight line for so long they found it impossible to side step one another and with all the shaking of hands and searching for friends the whole thing took on the confusion of a drunken slow motion eight-some reel.

Not long after the race had finished and the athletes had warmed down one of the suited men clapped his hands and shouted, "Come, come!" Everyone gathered under one of those squashed looking trees whose big branches and leaves protected us from the sun. Without anyone telling them what to do, the runners crouched or sat cross legged in large semi-circles like primary school children waiting to be told a story. Grouped together they gave off a smell of fresh sweat, sweet like decomposing woodchips. A P.A. system running off a generator that coughed softly in the background had been put in place and a well dressed woman with a medallion round her neck stepped forward. She spoke into the microphone in Kiswahili for twenty minutes even though it was clearly not working. I didn't understand a word but had an impression that it was some sort of pep talk. Every so often the audience laughed and I laughed too. So did Mike. Then he would catch my eye and we'd laugh even harder. Over at the finishing area, Gideon, the man who was almost certainly Paul Tergat and a couple of other senior looking runners were putting discarded water bottles into bin bags. The woman wound up to a grand finale and everyone applauded. She handed the broken microphone to an older man. The generator cleared its throat and the man started speaking.

"You must remember," he warned the athletes, "that you run first for God, second for the glory of Kenya and third for yourself."

"He is worried about more athletes defecting to other countries," Gideon whispered. "Some of these other men in suits are agents."

The man with the malfunctioning microphone continued to encourage the runners to train hard and not have their heads turned by worldly distractions. He went on telling a group of probably the most motivated runners in the world this message for thirty minutes.

"I hate all this." Gideon grimaced. "I hate it but I really miss it as well."

"Now let me invite a runner who needs no introduction," the suit shouted into the broken microphone, "a man who ran here as a youth and still comes here to train, even though he has achieved greatness all over the world."

The lanky, graceful man who must surely have been Paul Tergat ambled to the front, smiling humbly at his trainers as the audience applauded. Mike took photos while the male and female winners with a mixture of pride and shyness were presented with their flight tickets and travel money. The crowd, all of whom had competed fiercely for the same prize, whistled and cheered their approval.

"There is no place like this," Gideon continued. "I live in Nairobi because of my wife's work and to be close to her people. There are good runners there and we train hard but there is not the same community. Some of the runners here will not have seen their family for six months, maybe a year. That is just one of the sacrifices they have made."

"Could you not come here and train?"

"I think about it. Every time I return to Iten I'm filled with this enthusiasm. But it wouldn't be the same. I wouldn't share a room with four other men, struggling to get my kit washed and dried before the next training session. I would have my house, my car, my TV and sound system. I studied in America and became used to living like an American. How then should I be hungry?"

"But what about the greats, the runners who have achieved everything and stay at the top?"

"For me, these are the special ones. People like my father who never forgot where he came from and continued to live simply. Maybe in the days before big money could be made it was simpler. Tell me, what about your father, he was a great runner, an Olympian? Did he have to struggle with hardships as a young man?"

"No, not at all. He came from a wealthy family, went to University, trained to be a lawyer."

"And all this time he was running? Why?"

"Well, I think he just liked competing – or maybe more than that, he liked winning. He still does."

"This is very strange. You mean to say your father runs even today? Excuse me but he must be an old man. I have seen this often in America. Why does he do this to himself?"

I didn't know the answer, and shrugged. Gideon continued, "Me, when I retire I am going to get super fat and enjoy life. If I have enough money, of course." We all laughed at the idea of him becoming fat, but he was only half joking. "Mike, what about your father, is he also a great runner?"

"No," Mike mumbled, "my dad couldn't run the length of himself."

I thought of Mr Wetherson watching his son race. He couldn't get around much because a traffic accident had badly damaged his legs when he was still a young man. At Cross Countries or Road Races he would haul himself up to the highest point and stand there smoking, dressed as if he had just come in from gardening, with his muddy kneed cords and ill fitting cardigans. He didn't fit in with the other parents, many of whom were runners themselves and bounded about in expensive tracksuits bawling encouragement. He never clapped or shouted but drove Mike to every race, smiling ironically as his son won. Once when I was ten I had gone up to him and told him to put out his cigarette. He hadn't been standing within 30 metres of anyone and there was a spiteful wind. He stamped the cigarette out quickly on the ground and apologised to me. It was the first time an adult had ever sincerely apologised to me. I had skipped back to my mother to tell her what I had done.

"Oh well, you are the lucky one," Gideon said after some thought.

The winner of the men's race had been standing by Gideon's side while we were having this conversation. Now that we had stopped he touched the pace-maker's elbow. He spoke Kiswahili in a soft voice, leaning close to Gideon.

"Ah, this man wishes to ask a favour. He noticed you taking photos and wondered if you could send him the pictures."

"Of course," Mike agreed.

The tall race winner spoke and Gideon translated. "But he doesn't have access to the internet." They conferred for a minute before Gideon produced a pen and address book. "He wants to know if you could print the photos and post them to his mother's house?" Mike nodded an agreement and the man beamed at him. "But he doesn't know how to write the address," Gideon huffed in exasperation at the runner's pathetic attempt to make sensible letters appear on the page before intervening on his behalf. "There you are." He ripped the page out of his book and gave it to Mike.

"Have you put that somewhere safe?" I asked watching him fold the paper into his pocket.

"I am not a total monster."

There was an embarrassing silence until Gideon intervened. "Right we must go into town to meet that evil little brother of mine." As we walked Gideon pointed out a hotel high on a lush hill next to the town. "This is the work of another famous runner from Iten. The town is small but it has a number of fine hotels. The athletes also invest in schools and restaurants. Running drives the economy of this place, it is by far and away the biggest export."

"But that looks like a pretty fancy hotel, who can afford to stay there?"

"People like you." Gideon laughed. "Westerners who want to come here because they think they can learn how to run from us."

We spotted Moses loading the jeep with poly bags. He was talking to an elderly white man who I figured must be the fabled Father O'Grady.

"Who won?" The priest asked. After a great deal of debate about the actual names of the winners Mike settled it by showing Father O'Grady the photos he'd taken. "I don't know this one, but Janet was a former pupil of mine." He beamed proudly at the picture. "But isn't this just the thing," he said, looking at the camera from all angles as if this would help him understand it better.

"My school is just around the corner if you would like to pay it a visit." He removed his dog collar and released his top button. "That's better, praise the Lord."

The school was a little older than Mr K's in Eldoret but had been constructed with the same breeze blocks, and the same red corrugated iron roofing. After the classrooms with their enormous number of Victorian looking wooden desks and chairs, we arrived at the main hall. "Here we have a roll call of the champions from each school year." On a wooden panel affixed to the back wall were inscribed the names of Kenyan runners, a number of whom had gone on to do great things in the athletics world. "And here are our photos. To be sure we don't have a camera like yours, young Mike."

The photos were all in sepia and had faded from the sunlight that poured through the windows.

"There are some rare runners here," Father O'Grady said, letting Mike get on with the task of identifying which of the boys and girls in the photos had gone on to win Olympic medals and break World Records.

You could see Mike was totally psyched by all this. He started taking photos of photos. Father O'Grady thumbed through a battered pocket-sized Bible, trying to conceal the pride that was blooming on his face.

"I'll send you the shots I took of the woman, Janet, who won today. Colour photos," offered Mike.

"Well that would never do," replied the Priest, squinting at the display. "It would destroy the general aesthetic and besides, she hasn't won anything important, yet."

I could see what he meant. The photos on the wall all had the same cursive handwriting beneath them, naming the sepia runners who looked like they were from some distant, heroic past.

As we left the school I said, "Well, I wouldn't mind some of your photos. My camera was in the bag that got stolen."

"Do you not think you'll get that back? The police seemed to know who the criminal was."

"I hope I never see those policemen again."

"But your bag …"

"Is just a bag and the things inside it aren't important. Other than the photos stored on the camera, there was nothing I can't replace."

He stopped, his face suddenly slack with shock. "Shit. Your camera. What if they find it and look at that film you took. Christ, we'd be fucked. You'd be fucked."

"Yeah, thanks for giving them my name and all."

"I didn't realise."

"Did they get your journal?"

"No, I've still got that."

"Hopefully we can miss them."

"Well we're out of here in six hours. I can't wait to get going."

"I'm sure you can't."

"Well, don't pretend you want to stay. You were desperate to leave last night. Why can't you just admit that you want to go home, that you'll be happier away from all this?"

There were about a hundred things I wanted to say but all I managed was, "Why do you want me to admit that?"

"Because it's true."

"You don't understand anything."

"I understand that your little acts of charity are like putting a band-aid on a decapitated man. I also understand that you hate me and the fact that I'm here to get the most out of the training opportunities, instead of swanning around trying to save the world."

"Oooft," Moses said as if he'd seen a knockout blow.

"Eeek," screeched Gideon as if he'd seen a crunching tackle.

Looking round I realised we'd been standing, arguing, 10 metres from the jeep and were providing fine entertainment for our friends and a dozen passers-by. Mike blushed and I felt my cheeks tingle. The pedestrians crowded closer.

"Come on, a united front for now at least."

And, like some lackey, I followed him to the jeep. As we drove home the vehicle filled with the sweet chestnut smell of the runners' sweat. Sylvia and Faith slept and Moses cracked open his window. It was then as we passed one of the training camps that we heard the voices of female runners singing a gospel hymn. There were half a dozen of them sitting out on the grass, each with a basin of water and cumulous bubbles between their long black legs. Each scrubbed, and rubbed clothing from this morning's race before pegging the vests and shorts on a rope between two trees. There they fluttered in the light breeze, beautiful as bunting.

Alfred turned from the passenger's seat and noticing that we were both looking out the window said, "When you spread things out in the sun they become dry." He checked in my eyes to see that I had understood.

I opened my window and stuck out my head. The wind ruffled my short hair and I saluted the women even though they couldn't see me. Run, eat, sleep and repeat. That's what we thought their life was but I knew it wasn't that simple. Nothing ever is.

Chapter Seven

The Christian Cow greeted our return with a mournful moo. She looked as if she had realised something was up, that she couldn't have it this good forever. After packing the rest of my suitcase, I got ready for my final run. I like to shave before running. There's something about the air rushing past smooth cheeks that just feels good. After that I put Vaseline between my toes and plasters over my nipples. Finally I splashed on some aftershave. This wasn't just because I wanted to smell good but also because the stinging sensation made me feel more alive when I ran.

I did my stretches out the back with Moses and the two Americans. Then I put on my Ray-bans and asked Forrest if he could take photos of the rest of us running up the track to the Ks' farmstead.

"Could we not do it after the run, those clouds are looking ominous?"

"No, let's do it when we're fresh, it'll look better."

It didn't. With our mouths closed, brave looks on our dry faces, high knees and arms, we looked like runners in adverts for trainers. We did a fartlek session round a 12km route that I'd run round at least 50 times since arriving here. I can walk down a road that I train on regularly in Glasgow and think to myself but here's *an old church* or *when did that rusty gasworks appear?* Yet when running I'll know instinctively which paving stones wobble or the sequence of traffic lights at a cross roads.

Out here it was the same. I moved to the side of the road, watching the Americans run through a deceptively sticky stretch of mud that never dried. I knew which stones were safe as we skipped across a stream. But when Moses commented that the telephone poles had been cut down or pointed out three huts that looked to have been torched I had no idea if these were recent developments or not.

So on this, my final run, I tried to see and feel everything. With the bittersweet perspective of someone about to leave I realised that I had passed through this country with a tunnel vision, knowing where to place my feet and what obstacles to avoid but little else. I sprinted when it was time for us to sprint and jogged with the others to recover but it didn't seem important that my efforts were faster than theirs. At the end of the run the Americans shook my hand and wished me well, while the Christian Cow with its gentle face paced uneasily in the background.

My pulse had reached 222 BPM at the end of the last effort. Three minutes into the recovery run it had still been going at 145. I logged these times and noted that my legs had felt heavy, that I had fatigued rectus femoris, probably from all the cycling and squats I had been doing.

In mid-afternoon when the children and Kirsten had returned from school we had our going away party. The little girls all wore dresses and the boys wore shirts and bow ties that were held in place by an elastic band going round their necks. These were a bully's delight, great for being pulled so they pinged back at the wearer or twisted so that they spun. Once Gladys entered the room however, such behaviour stopped.

Kirsten and I had pride of place on the best sofa in the sitting room. I was wearing a shiny and synthetic counterfeit Kenyan Athletic Team track suit that I'd bought in the local market, while Kirsten was dressed in some Maasai rags and about a hundred bead necklaces given to her by the children.

"You look ridiculous, really."

"We both do," she assured me.

The children arrived from the dining area, dragging seats behind them for the adults and older children.

"Do you have your camera?" Gladys asked. I held it up.

"Great, please take many pictures and send them to us when you get home. It will mean so much to the children."

The first performance was an interpretation of a fairy tale, with Sammy as an over-enthusiastic wolf, Irene as a Little Red Riding Hood who seemed to know a few martial arts moves, and Kirsten as the exasperated director. It was a great success. Then came 'Crazy in Love' and a group of nine year olds dancing disturbingly like Beyoncé. After this a slightly older boy, who I had never seen speak to anyone, walked into the room to the starting bass of Billie Jean. He stood tapping his feet and I thought what was about to follow would be embarrassing for all but instead he moonwalked and struck poses across the varnished floor with the cool composure of someone that knows what they're doing is good. Embarrassment was never far away though and the whole room, with Kirsten the loudest, was soon insisting that I took to the floor.

"I'm sorry but I really can't dance," I told anyone who might be listening.

But Alfred, in that serious way of his, said, "Come, bad dancing does not break an engagement."

So, I was up there and the music had started and again I suspected Kirsten had a hand in this as the first notes of Shaggy's, 'Mr Boombastic' became recognizable. Three minutes of shaking and gyrating like a pervert uncle with rickets and I was back on the sofa red-faced and sweating, with Gladys still laughing so hard that tears were rolling down her face.

"Let's show him how it's done." Moses started pulling up the others. "Only a baboon laughs at the buttocks of another baboon." And so for the next ten minutes the whole assembly, from Gladys and Agnes the cook right down to the youngest child, danced. Joyce pronounced the whole scene to be "so uncool," but even she got up to dance. I felt exhausted from my efforts and took photos. I haven't seen those photos for years, but they were very beautiful, the children in their best clothes, their skin glowing and bright white teeth beaming, filled with an abandoned happiness that you rarely see in British kids.

The best photo of the bunch was one that someone had taken of me dancing. Eyes squeezed tight, even in a static pose I was obviously stiff and awkward. But it was the background, the little orphans laughing and holding onto each other, the kitchen women covering their mouths to prevent people seeing their bad teeth as they giggled, everywhere this mad glee taking place in a room full of glass cases containing running trophies and walls covered in framed photographs from IOCC events, the great and the good of world sport over the last few decades, serious and suited, looking down sternly on us. I deleted the photo the moment I got the chance. I shouldn't have; it was probably the one moment that I brought any joy to that country.

After the adults had danced themselves to a standstill we were ushered through to the dining room where Agnes's cake waited. She and the rest of the kitchen staff wrung their hands nervously until we pronounced it a success. It was in fact the sweetest cake I'd ever tasted. Whether this was because I wasn't used to eating sugary food anymore or it was just how they did it in Kenya I never knew. The little ones broke out the Monopoly board and, sugar-highed and shifty-eyed, played a game even more fractious and fraudulent than normal.

The TV came on and the adults shuffled back into the big Sitting Room to finish our cakes. The news was ending with some politicians giving speeches.

"Who are these guys?" I asked Moses.

Astonished, he replied, "This is Odaiga who we hope will be our next leader, the other is Kibaki, the current President."

Kirsten had gone off somewhere after eating the cake, but returned looking pale and smelling of mouthwash.

"Looking at their faces, I don't trust either of them," she said to no one in particular. "Have you ever had that feeling when looking at electoral posters abroad that even after hundreds of shots and airbrushing the photographer isn't able to hide the essential sleaziness of these characters' faces?"

I cleared my throat by way of saying *please stop*. She looked directly at me and explained.

"It's not that I think British politicians look any more trustworthy, just that we become so used to their fake smiles and cold eyes that we forget what we originally thought when we first saw them avoiding questions and telling lies."

"Odaiga is a far better man," said Moses. "He will break the Mount Kenya Mafia and there may even be less corruption. Do you know this Kibaki wanted to earn $40,000 a month for being President? That in a country where half the population make less than a dollar a day!"

His mother shook her head and, watching the crowd cheer at the Odaiga rally, said, "For me, all I know is that it is the grass that suffers when two elephants fight."

After the news came an end-of-year sports review. 90% of the programme was dedicated to distance running. There was a big roundup of the summer's World Championships in which Kenya had come second only to the United States in the medal table. It's hard to overstate how proud a country like Kenya is when it sees itself achieving great things on the world stage. Watching the 800 metres and marathon in which Kenya had won gold in both the men's and women's event sent a shiver through me. Even though the races were four months ago and everyone in that room knew the results they watched as if it was live, shouting the athletes' names and squealing as they crossed the line. Even the children momentarily abandoned their game of monopoly to contribute to the commotion. The 5000 metres was more controversial with Bernard Legat, a Kenyan who had taken American citizenship, beating Kipchoge in a sprint finish. The room filled with boos and shouts of 'traitor!' Alfred left after this, which surprised me because he loved his running. When he left Moses said, "We should not boo, it is after all a Kalenjin one – two."

"It is a Kenyan one – two," his mother corrected him.

The programme finished with the customary clean sweep of

the medals in the men's steeplechase. It seemed a fitting note on which to leave.

"Mr K will drive you to the bus station," announced Gladys. We collected our bags, and at the door she said, "It has been a real pleasure to have you, really, you have been no problem at all. Please tell all of your running friends about this place. Once the accommodation is finished we want to have athletes from the rest of the world come and train with our Kenyan runners. It is good for everyone, and it will help us buy food and clothes for the children."

Kirsten embraced the lady and I shook her hand.

The children danced about, shaking our hands and saying, "How do you do?" and "Nice to meet you," in that very proper English voice they tried to teach them in school. Kirsten as usual was kissing their heads and pinching their cheeks but they seemed more interested in being lifted up so they could hang from some metal railings that were used to dry clothes on.

After saying goodbye to the family I exchanged another variation on one of those complicated handshakes that I never quite got the grip of with Moses who said, "Keep strong," before beating his chest with his fist. His final words were, "Watch out for the Tigers in Mombasa, though I'm sure Kirsten will keep a close eye on you." These words didn't make much sense as there weren't any tigers in Mombasa or anywhere else in Africa. I looked for Alfred in the hope he would explain what his friend meant, but he was nowhere to be seen. Kirsten noted their email addresses in her journal, and promised we would communicate by that. Sometimes I have wondered if she was sincere, but we in the west have lost the ability to say goodbye. Instead we say, I'll email you, knowing even as we are saying the words that we never will. And even if we do all that happens is that the bonds of friendship slowly rot and disintegrate instead of being cut when they're fresh.

The car appeared and I took a deep breath. I was overwhelmed by the prospect of being driven somewhere by an Olympic champion.

"Good evening sir," I said, "it has been an honour to stay in your house." Kirsten was still saying her goodbyes. "I'm really sorry about this."

"It's no problem, the children seem to like her." He turned the radio up louder. It was a news report about the election. Kirsten got in the car and did the sort of dignified sob that posh people and actresses do to show they have feelings. The car moved down the driveway and everyone waved. Everyone, that is, except the boys I had left hanging from the washing rails and forgotten to lift down. The light was quickly failing, and I felt a surge of elation at the thought that we were finally going home.

"There has been some trouble on the road between Eldoret and Mount Elgon. Many people are leaving their homes to go back to their tribal lands, but hopefully this will not affect our journey."

"Is this because they have to vote there?"

"No," Mr K chuckled mirthlessly, "that is not the problem."

We passed a great many more people on the road than was usual. Some pushed bikes laden with belongings or encouraged emaciated looking horses suffering under loads that looked heavier than themselves; others simply carried their belongings and children in shawls and cotton bags tied round their shoulders and necks. A woman with the type of walk that thousands of European models would kill for balanced belongings on her head, hips swaying, posture stately. Further down the road a bus with a ridiculous number of people sitting on its roof had become stuck or burst a tyre. We drove on as people climbed down the sides and reached out to the car, their pink palms and ping pong eyes caught in our headlights.

"Sometimes, but only sometimes, you have to drive on," said Mr K.

I wanted to ask him how it felt to win Olympic medals or about some of the famous sportsmen that I had seen him pictured with back in the farmstead, but Kirsten got in first. "Is this because of the election?"

"Yes, this type of thing happens before every election. Don't worry, I will make sure you get safely onto your bus."

I tried to remember what the two candidates Moses had been talking about were called but their names were just noise to me.

"Do you think the election will make any difference to the poor of this country?" asked Kirsten.

"Good question. Odaiga says he is the champion of the poor but for me nothing will change no matter who wins. Furthermore, leaders in African countries seldom lose power by the ballot box. We have a very interesting concept of democracy in this continent."

The two of them got into some big discussion about politics and my chance to ask what it felt like to have an Olympic medal hanging round your neck was lost.

Driving into Eldoret reminded me why I was so happy to be leaving this country and its horrible corrugated clutter, its open sewers and people sprawling about the road sides as if they had been trampled by a crowd and left to die. Mr K navigated round to the Bus Stop where two buses waited and a maelstrom of misery was kept in check by some officials with big sticks. Parking the car Mr K said, "Well this looks like a sorry mess."

Two street kids rushed over. "Mistah, we look after your car."

"The Alsatian on the back seat will do that just fine," lied Mr K.

"Yeah, but does your dog know how to blow up tyres?"

Mr K went over to the boys and spoke sternly to them in Kiswahili. After a minute or two he gave each of them what looked like a business card and patted their heads. "Come, come," he bade us, walking towards the bus. "It is good that you are not wearing any jewelry," he said to Kirsten, "but you, please remove your watches before boarding the bus. Your journey at this time in the evening should be safe but you will disembark quite late. Tourists do not call it Nairobbery for nothing."

There seemed no way through the crowd but at one nod from Mr K, two policemen started banging at people's shins with their sticks until a passage had cleared for us. Kirsten and I froze, thinking they were going to be part of the interrogation squad from the previous night. There was nowhere to run, but the policemen showed no sign of recognising us. Mr K pushed us gently forward, saying, "Go quickly, you have nothing to fear from the police." As we shuffled forward I tried to look at his face, to see if it betrayed the uncertainty that his shaking voice suggested.

"Remember, get a licensed taxi from the bus station to your hotel and bargain hard. Good journey," the great athlete said, "and please tell others about our training camp – and Kirsten, send my regards to your father."

Our tickets, which I remembered the man in the important hat saying were for the specialist seats, allowed us to sit directly behind the driver. Watching the other passengers climbing aboard carrying whole chickens that were not obviously dead, I thought this was a good thing. I gave Eldoret one final glance and spotted Mr K woodenly crossing the square, walking like a marathon runner the morning after the race. Striding towards him was the square-headed policeman flanked by two of his stave wielding enforcers. Mr K hailed the officer who, after speaking into his radio, eyeballed the legendary runner. The bus filled with those who had tickets whilst those begging and remonstrating with the officials were pushed from the closing doors. The engine started and I slithered low in my seat pulling Kirsten down.

"What?" she hissed.

As the bus swung out of the square I saw the officer pull a baton from his belt as Mr K shook his head. On a wall of the Kindness Barbers someone had chalked words in skeletal, capital letters. PEACE PLEASE. They would be washed off by the morning.

Chapter Eight

A driver wearing a Spitfire pilot's helmet, a chicken realising what peril it was in trying to fly from the bus despite clipped wings, a travelling companion who smelt like the transition zone of Boots and who insisted on wearing a face mask to protect his pure lungs from the diesel fumes that sneaked through the window. We rollercoasted towards the Nairobi road past the sprawling squalor of Eldoret's growing slums where raw sewage navigated a maze of narrow lanes, broken glass glinted on the top of every wall; where thousands of people somehow lived.

"The great escape," Mike gasped from behind his mask as we left the ragged edges of the city behind. "I thought those policemen were waiting for us. Anyway, you can relax now."

Relax? What I felt was an anticlimax: Malpas, the street children, the poor of this country, had I not let them down? Maybe I would have felt better if I had been arrested by the police.

"Maybe the police chief will call a station on the Nairobi Road and they'll set up a road block. Take us out into the scrub and shoot us."

Appalled, Mike pulled the surgical mask back over his face.

Across the aisle from us a pair of men dressed like university professors were getting stuck into a packed dinner and some cans of Tusker beer. I really wanted a drink or, even better, a smoke. And once that idea of getting totally brained had lodged in my head there was no shifting it. But it was impossible. The bus had No Smoking signs everywhere and was without a toilet.

The first section of the road to Nairobi climbed uphill to an even higher point of the Rift Valley. Our driver took great delight in overtaking trucks whose top speeds were only a couple of mile per hour slower than ours. On a two lane road with the occasional Matatu Minibus hurtling Kamikaze-like towards us this was certainly an alternative form of entertainment.

"Now I see why that man in the station office called these the specialist seats," said Mike. "They don't even have any seatbelts."

As if on cue, the driver slammed on the brakes and the bus shuddered down a gear to allow the passengers a glimpse of a Minibus crumpled like a stamped-on coke can.

Mike removed his face mask and, holding up a packet of Party Rings that he had obviously stored for this journey, asked, "Do you want a biscuit?"

I had puked up Agnes' cake almost as soon as I'd eaten it and my stomach felt the size of a child's fist. I declined.

"I can't wait to get to the hotel. Just think, proper food, a swimming pool and gym, hot showers!"

I smiled. The rest of it didn't bother me but I could stand under a hot shower for hours.

"It's a shame we didn't get to say goodbye to Alfred. I really liked him. Where do you think he was?" Mike asked whilst crunching through biscuits.

"I think he was probably hiding."

"Hiding?"

"Yeah, I think he felt uncomfortable with everyone booing Legat in that race we watched. His brother represented Qatar in the same Championships, remember? I think he's ashamed of this."

"Shit, I'd forgotten." Mike slapped his forehead. "Imagine having a brother who turned his back on his own country though. It'd make you feel pretty bad."

"It's a bit more complicated than that."

"Not really. I mean would you run for another country just because they offered you money?"

"It really wouldn't bother me. I can't understand why sportspeople are all meant to be great patriots. Waving a flag of some disintegrating Union or that represents a country that enslaved their forefathers. The national anthems are the worst part. I hate how newspapers and TV commentators love individuals who sing heartily along to some ode celebrating an old privileged woman whose life has nothing to do with 99% of her subjects."

"But you saw their reactions watching that highlights show. Sporting success makes a nation feel good about itself."

"I don't see why having the best sportspeople should make a country proud. Besides, the Kenyans already have enough runners to hold up as idols. You saw the level of competition today. Coming in the top three of the men's Steeplechase trials in this country is probably harder than doing it at the Olympics. You could be one of the fastest runners in the world but still never get to compete on the world stage."

"But they can't just become a factory exporting runners around the world. You've seen how much it means to the country when their runners win."

"I don't see why the nation should care. The obsession with medal tables is sick. I mean, most elite athletes are freaks, so being proud of having a culture that produces the most freaks is pretty fucked up."

"What do you mean they're freaks?"

"You should see the nick of most of the girls in the showers after an international cross country. I mean hollow hips, visible spines, they look like photos from the Holocaust."

"I still think it's damaging for Kenya to see its top runners, people that put the place on the map defect for financial reason."

"Alfred told me that his brother sent money to Mr K's orphanage and that he had helped put his other brother through university. You've seen how poor most of these people are. If some oil-rich state offers them a million dollars like they did with Saaeed Shaheen, a lifetime salary, that sort of thing, who are we to deny them?"

"But it's so shameful to watch. I mean Saaeed Shaheen

is really Stephen Cherono and his brother Abraham still runs for Kenya. When Shaheen wins a race he does a lap of honour wrapped in a flag he probably wouldn't have recognised 5 years earlier."

"I'm sorry, but in the general scheme of things there is a lot worse happening in the world."

And there we were. Stuck together but unable to do anything but argue. Mike sat back and snapped his face mask over his mouth. The wind hurtling through the driver's window made it too cold to sleep, and the fear of what was happening on the road ahead made it too frightening to pretend. Eventually we slowed down at the edge of some village whose name I would never know.

"Is there a road block?"

I peered out of the driver's window. Women balancing baskets on their heads loomed up to the bus, offering sweet corn and samosas wrapped in newspaper; bunches of bananas tapped at the window and the smell of spicy potato bhaji being cooked in pans of frying oil wafted through the night. All the transactions were done through the windows and the driver refused to let anyone off for a toilet break. Only when we were well past the village did he pull off the road at what looked like a massive abandoned car park and shout, "10 minutes!"

There were no actual toilets. This was preferable to squatting over the filthy, fly infested holes in the ground that made your eyes water and gut wrench. I clambered off the bus with Mike following.

"Where are you going?"

"For a piss. It's not really a spectator sport."

"I won't look, I'll just stand guard here. Have you got tissues?"

"Nah, I'll just drip dry."

Mike winced and turned his back on me as I skidded down a bank at the far end of the car park, hands already fumbling through my satchel for my vaporiser and bag of dope. It was pretty dark down there but I worked on automatic, stuffing clumps of weed into the heating compartment. I could hear movement in the undergrowth to one side of me, and a voice chatting to others in the dark with the camaraderie of men pissing outdoors. An arc of urine was caught momentarily in the moon's white light. The man walloped his willy about then buttoned himself back in. He hadn't seen me. The green light indicating optimum temperature came on and I inhaled like a person waking from a nightmare.

I sat down, wiping the cold sweat off my forehead. The idea of climbing further down that bank, or hill, or mountain and finding some long vegetation to lie in and smoke until I couldn't function was appallingly appealing. But I staggered to my feet and clawed my way back to the car park. I expected Mike to be waiting impatiently but he was nowhere to be seen. How long had I been gone? The buses were where I'd left them but the passengers had formed a big group at the far end of the car park. Someone shouted my name, so I walked in their direction. Mike grabbed me as I merged with the crowd.

"You have to see this, it's ridiculous, fraudulent!"

At one end of the car park was a cleaning area where you could attach a basin and wash yourself. A line of four orange plastic basins, two of which were filled with water, could be seen illuminated by a single hanging light bulb. A Kenyan man wearing a doctor's overcoat asked, "Which way will the water drain when I pull the plug?"

"Down?" I answered.

"No, I mean, will it swirl clockwise or anti-clockwise?"

Being someone that had spent a fair amount of time watching their vomit flush away down the toilet, I was pretty sure I knew the answer. "Clockwise," I shouted full of confidence.

"Correct," the Kenyan said. "Now come this way."

At the other side of the car park was a similar unit. The man strode purposefully to the basins, knowing that the people would follow. "And here," he said, "which way will the water swirl?"

"Anti-clockwise," suggested a few Kenyans from our bus. I couldn't see why this should be but as the man pulled the plug the water did in fact twist that way.

I couldn't believe my eyes. "How did that happen?" The man simply laughed and spread his hands out like a magician or a messiah. Mike pointed at a big sign that said EQUATOR. "So those sinks are in the northern hemisphere and we're in the south?"

"That's the idea."

The man collected a few shillings from each of us and bowed. I was full of questions. "But how does it work?"

"It is," said the Kenyan man, "to do with the spinning of the earth."

"I see," I replied, even though I didn't.

"What we saw was supposedly an example of the Coriolis effect," Mike explained once we were on the bus. "It's caused by the rotations of the earth and makes hurricanes in the North generally spiral anti-clockwise and those in the South clockwise."

"Did the water in the basin not go the other way?"

"Exactly," he said, watching the man in the doctor's coat give our driver a handshake in which a few notes seemed to be exchanged. "There are many things that will affect how water in something as small as a basin will rotate. For example, if the man poured the water in so that it originally rotated in a clockwise direction the water will remember this, even if he did it many minutes earlier and it appears still. When he pulls the plug it will drain in that direction."

"So it was a trick?"

"Sort of."

"But the equator?"

"Is somewhere around here to be sure but that sign probably doesn't mark the exact line. It's pretty convenient if it does."

"So that man moved the equator and water has a memory. Shit, this stuff is amazing."

Mike looked at me strangely before firing on about vectors

and torques and experimental conditions. But I'd heard all I needed to know, at least for now, and his prattling just confused me.

"Tell me another story," I begged. "Where are we right now? I mean, can you check are we North or South?"

He pulled out his guidebook and started reading.

"Well if we're in the South you should see Lake Nekuru to your right, famous for its population of flamingoes which are so numerous that they make the banks of the lake appear to be coloured pink when seen from a great distance. Fancy that Kirsten, flamingoes! Shame it's night time and the only things we can see are our own reflections and the occasional car wreck."

"I can see them but the flamingoes are definitely flying. What else is there?"

"Well there are white rhinos and, if you're very lucky, leopards."

"Haha, I can see them too, especially the very lucky leopards" I chuckled, cupping my hand so I could see out my window. "Look, a boa constrictor," I shouted before realising it was a shredded truck tyre.

"You don't get boas in Africa." Mike tutted.

But what did he know? At the moment I could have dragons and fairies in Africa if I wanted. We travelled through the great hills of the Rift Valley, over land that humans had lived on for a million years, through villages that looked like something that had been thrown together in the last couple of days. A little bus full of light and foreign smells rattling across a pitch black land. I gloried in the fact that no-one at home knew of my travel plans, that if we rolled down one of the drops at the roadside I might never be identified.

"You do realise that the first thing folks will ask when we get home is what animals have we seen. The Christian Cow isn't really going to impress anybody."

I knew he wasn't interested in seeing animals. We'd twice been asked if we wanted to go on Safari and both times he'd refused, saying the drop in altitude would ruin his research and reduce the benefit of all our training. Of course no-one had offered to take me, a white female with no companion, on my own.

"There's a crocodile farm in Mombasa. Why don't we go there?"

"Ok," I agreed, even though I hate seeing animals in captivity.

"Animals in a zoo sound much better. At least you know where they're going to be."

I think I must have dozed for the rest of the journey. I remembered waking with a jerk a couple of times and realising that I was using Mike's lap as a pillow and that my face had that awful, slack saggy feeling it got when I smoked. For his part he stared through the windscreen trying to spot roadblocks or to see the lights of a chasing police car in the wing mirror. At one point he must have put his jacket over my shoulders. Too weird, too freaky, him doing something like that.

Nairobi bus station just before midnight was not a place for sleepy thoughts. Mike slipped his penknife from his bag into his pocket. "Right," he said, "no one's going to make a muggery out of us."

In a country where people regularly carried machetes and vicious looking work tools I didn't feel entirely reassured. From above, the bus station must have looked like a great and confusing game of Tetris, as colourful buses, taxis and Matatus negotiated for space. The walls were covered with the same election posters as in Eldoret. During the day people put them up and at night they were defaced or half ripped from the wall so the politicians appeared ghoulish creatures with peeling faces and horns on their heads. Lots of people tried to attract our attention with shouts, of "Hey, hey, you!" but we humped our backpacks to the nearest taxi. It was a greyish colour with the same yellow stripe down one side that all the taxis had so I was happy to get in; but Mike held me back.

"How much to The H?" He asked through the window.

The driver drummed on his steering wheel and shrugged impressively before saying, "1000 shillings."

"1000 shillings. You've got to be joking?"

1000 shillings was about $10. Not a lot in the grand scheme of things but clearly a rip-off out here. The driver continued drumming and staring through his windscreen. He was digging his music and could sit here all night chilling: that was what he wanted us to know. We on the other were carrying heavy backpacks and had to cross this unknown city at night. But there were at least twenty other taxis waiting, and when there is choice the consumer is king – that, at least, was what Mike thought.

"How much to the H?" Mike asked the next driver.

"The same as what he said."

We walked to another part of the bus station. "Excuse me but how much to the H?"

"1200 shillings."

Mike guffawed, convincingly this time, and claimed, "The driver over there said 800."

"The price of gas has gone up."

"What, in the last 5 minutes?"

"Ok, ok," the man relented, "you can promote me. How is 700 shillings?"

"300."

The man shook his head and said, "You are wasting my time." But there were no other fares there. Mike turned to walk away and I was just about to say, 'Fuck it, I'll pay,' when the man said, "Ok, 500."

"We have been living at the home of the famous athlete K, teaching at his school and helping build housing for orphans of this country," Mike ranted, somewhat exaggerating our contributions to Kenyan life.

The man shrugged. "What are you talking about? What should I care about these things?"

Mike grunted in disgust and got in. The man made a similar

119

noise and started his engine. The cab was pretty old with black leather seats covered by a white doily type of rug. Hanging from his wing mirror was a variety of beads, Christian crosses and other religious icons. The driver caught my reflection looking at them and said, "So you are staying in The H, what a nice and fantastic hotel."

"I wouldn't know," I replied, "I've never been before."

"Then let me give you some advices. Tomorrow I will make you a grand tour of the city. Other people will offer their service but they will only try and steal your money. You can't trust no-one in this town."

Mike rolled his eyes as the taxi beeped and sneaked its way across a cross roads. There seemed to be no traffic lights or indeed order in the way people drove. Matatu minibuses were even more garishly painted than in Eldoret. We only narrowly avoided colliding into the back of one which was devoted to Liverpool FC and had a greenish tinged mural of Steven Gerard playing football in Space on the back doors.

The Nairobi H was surrounded by other hotels and the head offices of a number of multi-national companies. A brightly lit, cylindrical skyscraper, it was the biggest building I'd seen in months. Both of us stood on the pavement looking at it with something like awe.

"We could be in Europe or America," Mike said.

This was the type of comment I was to hear a lot there. Usually it was said approvingly along with words such as 'oasis' and 'godsend'. Occasionally you heard someone new to the country complaining that they wanted something more authentic, whilst those who had been out *roughing it* on Safari tours squealed loudly to each other about flushing toilets and silver service.

Neither of us could really afford it but Moses, who had organised the trip, had insisted. The cost of one night's stay would be more than we'd probably spent in our previous three months, which was pretty sickening, but Mike was clearly excited and had kept saying that we deserved a treat. The reception had a marble floor – good for clicking important shoes across – and was brightly lit without there being any obvious source of lights. The staff stood cardboard-cutout still. A real Christmas tree had been flown in from somewhere and was tastefully decorated with white lights and Victorian style baubles. It could have been any H in the world apart from the X-ray machine that our bags had to go through. The receptionist rested his tapered fingers on the desk as if he was about to play a beautiful concerto. He asked for our names and passports and gave us a key. "Where's the other key?"

"Moses has probably booked us into a twin room," Mike suggested.

He headed for the lifts giggling like he had pulled off some huge coup. You have to remember, we were only nineteen and the idea of staying in a hotel alone, let alone the H, after three months roughing it, was pretty exciting. "I thought they would knock us back because we weren't dressed right or something, I've never stayed in a place like this before," Mike gabbled. "Let's go and see if the swimming pool is open, or the restaurant! I'm going to eat so much."

"It's after midnight, shouldn't we try and get some sleep?"

"But there'll be other people from Britain here. Tourists who won't speak such horrible English."

The lift stopped at the eighteenth floor. "Listen, I'm pretty beat. I'll see you for breakfast in the morning. Don't do anything too crazy."

"Come on, we could even get a beer and look out over this city." He stalked me with a crazy look in his eyes. Mike and beer? I couldn't think of anyone less interested in drinking. "They'll probably have Wi-Fi and Sky Sports on the telly," he shouted as the lift doors closed on him.

"I'm going to have a shower so won't hear the door for half an hour," I shouted back.

I was psyched by the privacy of a room with a lock on the door. At K's I was always a guest, worrying that Agnes might come in to clean the room or that Joyce would poke her head round the door. With Mike out of the way I doubted there'd be any distractions. I'd become quite used to being in bed by 9.30 as part of the training camp regime so hadn't been lying to Mike when I said I was tired. But even so I went through to the bathroom with my vaporiser, worried that he wouldn't be gone long on his own. The bathroom light activated an extractor fan and I turned the shower on to further hide any suspicious smells. I waited until it had steamed up all the mirrors and I wouldn't have to see myself then took hit after hit from the vaporiser. White tiled walls, behind two locked doors in an anonymous room in a city where only one other person knew my name. I climbed into the shower, turned the heat up so it was scaldingly hot, and sat on the dimpled porcelain floor. The water patted my head and filled my eyes and ears and nose. I washed my short hair again and again until I was covered with bubbles. The shampoo had some sort of mint extract in it which stung my eyes and made my scalp tingle. I could laugh or I could cry and no one would know any different.

The bed I crawled into was so high above the streets that the squabble of traffic and late night traders couldn't possibly reach my ears. I sank my head into the pillow's paunch and twisted the sheets around me.

I must have slept, for a voice shouting, "Kirsten, please open up, I can't sleep in the corridor," sounded through the door. Shit, he must have been there for ages if he had taken to shouting. I scurried towards the door before realising I was naked. I grabbed a sheet, wrapped it round my body and unclipped the lock, trying to sprint back to bed before he saw me.

"Christ, there's only one bed," was the first thing he said. I pretended to be sleeping which was pretty lame considering I'd just opened the door. "Well, I suppose I should just get a few towels and sleep on the floor," he mused out loud, as if I couldn't hear. "I guess there should be enough room for me down here and the carpet doesn't look too uncomfortable. Shame there isn't a mosquito net though."

"You can sleep in the bed," I muttered keeping my head

buried. "Sorry I didn't open the door, I'm a little bit naked."

"Oh, ok, I quite understand. Well if you're sure."

I felt the weight of someone else on the mattress and another body not moving, breathing in measured gasps, unobtrusive as a ventilator. I guess we lay there like two stiffs for some time. I was wrapped tight in sheets while he kept his clothes on. Both of us pretended to be asleep. But eventually I must have dozed off for I dreamt I was running over a Highland heath and that it was snowing heavily until the hills and the great continents of clouds became one colour. I couldn't stop stumbling, and my shoes were poorly tied and I wasn't wearing the right clothes. Other people, perhaps wearing skis, repeated themselves in the distance but they were as uninvolved in the narrative as the background scenery in a cartoon race. The snow fell softly on my shoulders and cartwheeled down my skin with a touch as light as dandelion pollen. I gave up on the running and curled up in a foetal position in the snow. A comforting warmth enfolded me and I realised something no one else ever had – snow is warm. I felt its fingers run down the small hairs beneath my belly button, then up to strum my jutting ribs before kneading the dip in my side above my hips. I must have slept back to that moorland, only now I knew that I had lost something on it which I shouldn't have, a baby or young child I think, and there was no way I was going to find it. So I curled tight in the snow until I was comfortably buried. I woke up scrabbling with the folds of mosquito netting, forgetting already what I had lost, what I should have been searching for.

Mike wasn't in the bed and I had no way of telling the time, so I got dressed quickly and rushed down to breakfast. It was astonishing to see so many Westerners. I couldn't help eavesdropping on their conversations but felt shy and somehow ashamed around them. Mike had commandeered a small table and waved me over.

"I've done a circuit in the gym already," he announced. "I tried the running machine as well but it sort of broke my heart. You know, running on the spot in some air-conditioned room with Abba playing in the background. It's just not the same. And all these fat people bouncing about, looking at their jiggly bits in the mirror as if by staring they could magic them away." He made a disgusted face that showed all the disdain an elite runner can muster towards the part time jogger. "Some of them weren't even sweating."

The buffet was pretty incredible. I massaged my caved-in stomach. The smell of fried bacon after meatless months was pretty irresistible. If Mike hadn't been there I'd probably have given in. But his delight would have been too much. So I piled my plate up high with scrambled eggs, fried tomatoes and mushroom.

Mike grinned and said, "Get stuck in," before going and collecting second helpings. I watched him from behind. He was wearing a T-shirt, tight enough to show off his physique. Low slung jeans that let everyone know that his boxer shorts were of an expensive Italian brand. Hair neatly gelled, strong, fresh-faced, captain of the team, lead male looks. I was seeing him the way three or four other women in the restaurant were seeing him. I felt a little unlocked to think I had lain in bed, naked in the light of the morning as he got ready for the gym

At the table next to us sat a pensionable playboy with white hair swept back into a pony tail and a face wrinkled and ravaged as a dried out lake bed. Across from him a petite African girl who looked about my age, perched with perfect poise forking cut up bits of grapefruit into her lovely mouth. He was eating smoked kippers, and when not spitting bones out onto his hands kept reaching out and stroking the shiny smooth skin on her upper arms. In a cockney voice he cajoled and gently mocked her the way some men do when they think they are courting. I tried to eat some of my mushrooms but even after chewing for a couple of minutes found it hard to keep them down. Yogurt. That's what I should have gone for. Expands the stomach if you haven't eaten much for some time.

"What about the swimming pool?" I asked, looking out the restaurant window. "Looks pretty nice."

"I don't know, I heard some woman say it was dirty, and I mean, even in a place like this there're all sorts of waterborne diseases you could pick up."

"Well, I fancy a dip later on."

I continued chewing and attempting to digest my fry-up. So much greasy food after a period of eating nothing but cereals and vegetables was disgusting but I knew I was going to throw up once I got back to my room.

White American couples kept coming into the room holding one or in some cases two Kenyan babies. They all seemed to know each other but had broken down into family units. The men held the babies as if they were dangerous as bombs, fragile as bouquets of flowers. For the most part they looked ill at ease, checking to see if anyone was watching. The women seemed more comfortable; sated, you could almost say. The crying of little humans not able to express their desires or fears started to fill the room. The playboy wiped his fingers and got up. The Kenyan girl silently followed.

"I fucking hate cockneys," Mike said.

I agreed even though we both knew it wasn't what he meant.

After breakfast I went up stairs to shave and shower. I looked at myself naked in a full length mirror for the first time in ages. The blonde hairs on my legs probably hadn't been this long since I was eleven and I suddenly felt embarrassed about having gone about like this for weeks. My arms, legs and face were all quite tanned which made the hairy bits even more obvious. The rest of me was fungal white. I shoogled my breasts and squeezed the tops of my thighs. As I touched my body I remembered the fingers feeling me last night. There was nothing sexual about the memory. The fingers seemed as sensual as a doctor or butcher, measuring, checking, pinching my fat.

I was glad I had a full body swimming costume. My belly looked swollen from the disgusting breakfast I had gorged on.

After turning the shower on to conceal any noises I checked the door was locked. Mike was away looking up things on the internet so I was safe for now. I folded a towel on the floor and knelt on it before thrusting two fingers into the back of my throat. I boaked and my eyes watered but before I had a chance to catch my breath I was back at it. I gagged again. A string of acrid phlegm hung from my hand and stomach acid stung the back of my nose. I thought of the glistening succulent tomatoes, greasy mushrooms, soaking up egg yolk with my toast. I retched, my knees coming off the floor and hands gripping the side of the bowl as I spewed. The first round of vomiting got rid of all the heavy stuff. After that it was easy. I made myself sick four more times sipping water so the vomit that came up was still cold. I rested my head on the toilet bowl then blew my nose and flushed.

The mirror had steamed up again. I brushed my teeth and gargled cold minty water. The back of my throat felt like someone had been grinding glass on it. I clawed my fingers across the condensation of the mirror then let them touch my face.

"Never again lardy legs," I whispered. "Never let me catch you eating something like that again."

After my shower I put my swimming costume on under a T-shirt and shorts. The pool was quiet at that time of the day, apart from a few of the new parents seeing if their adopted babies would take to water. It was a sunny day and with Nairobi being much lower than where we had been living the air temperature was warmer. I thought I might get cramp in my calf muscles, so I did a few stretches before lying back and supping on a bottle of water.

Two ladies, pink and green bikinis but both with bottle blonde hair and Oompa-Loompa tans reclined on loungers, just out of earshot you would say if they spoke at a normal volume. Each had cocktails the colour of their bikinis. They drank from these with straws, their made up lips forming a perfect O as they did so. I could tell that they had observed my arrival and were commenting on me with their eyes.

"Well, after that Safari it's good to get back to the basic

necessities," brayed Green Bikini.

"I should say. You wouldn't even know you were in Africa."

"But it's not really the standard of a Western H."

"No, there's a damp area on one of our walls and Freddy found a hair in the shower."

"Still, what can you expect?"

"It's safe, that's the main thing."

"Have you been out *there*?" She whispered the final word.

"Not much but Freddy says it's quite safe during the day. This country's really quite a success. I mean the people get along for the most part."

"Well of course, they're not savages."

"Dedan, Dedan! Be a dear and fix us two more cocktails. Yes, that's right, the same again."

And so it went. The pool was on a large terrace maybe 5 or 6 storeys above street level. From here you'd probably have a pretty good view of Nairobi but there were perfectly pruned hedges around the whole area. I really wanted to cool down in the pool but felt self-conscious about swimming in front of those two. On the other hand I could hardly lie there for ten minutes and then retreat. So I stuck it out before pretending to rummage through my rucksack, sighing pointedly at not finding whatever I was apparently searching for before nipping back into the hotel.

I met Mike at the computers. "So what's happening in the world?"

"Well on the 18th December, 2007 I can report that it was minus 5 last night in Glasgow, Johnny said he and Andrew both did a sub 30, 10km time trial but I know the route they ran starts at a higher point than it ends, and there's some sort of problem with refuse collection in Naples."

"Momentous. It's your birthday isn't it – sorry, I forgot."

"Don't worry about it. I'll celebrate when I get home."

"No, we should do something tonight in Mombasa."

"Yeah well, why not. I met an American couple who are getting the same bus as us. We're going to get a taxi to the bus station together. Apparently they usually pay 400 shillings."

He went up to our rooms to collect our bags and I stayed to check my emails. Mike's dad had sent me a message which was something that had never happened before.

Hi Kirsten

How are you two doing out there? I know it's difficult for you to find computers with internet access but if you get this can you say, "Happy Birthday," to Mike from me. Tell him his Gran is going to bake him a cake for his return. I've written to him four or five times but haven't had a reply for a couple of weeks, but I know you're both very busy training. There was a report on the news of rioting and people being displaced in Kenya but we couldn't make out where this was happening. Have you seen any of this? There haven't been any follow up reports so it's probably nothing too serious. We had the first snow of the winter today. Scotland will seem very dull and cold I imagine. Everyone is very proud of the two of you. Hope you get the most out of your last few days, I'll see you both at the airport.

Much love, Steve

I read this a couple of times, thinking about Mike's dad driving him up and down the country to races; watching in his jumble sale assortment of clothes as his boy, in luminous spikes and branded running gear, raced to victory. It made me want to cry. The misplaced pride of parents: there's not much sadder than that. Mike came down carrying a backpack in each hand, his forearms bulging, and I quickly logged off.

On the road waited the usual line of taxis you get in front of any international hotel. The drivers shouted and gesticulated with twirling fingers. They were nervous about the porters though and never shouted too loudly or came too close. The street children were more daring: they had to be. They carried the same old shoe boxes containing their wares, a couple of packets of chewing gum and tissues. Even the pots of glue that they clung to were the same. I almost expected Malpas or the cute boy in the denim jacket to step forward, smiling as if to say, *you didn't think you would get away that easily?*

"You, hello, you, hoo-wah-yooo?"

"Scussi non capito, sono Italiano, non parlo Inglese," Mike said winking at me.

"Va bene, ciao, buongiorno come stai?" said the tallest of the street kids.

"Shit, that's me stuck. These ones are a bit cosmopolitan."

The bikini girls from the swimming pool appeared, behind Ascot hats and oversized sunglasses. For a moment I panicked, thinking it was they who Mike had befriended, but that was clearly impossible.

"Look at the children, Jacqueline, aren't they adorable?"

"I gave one of those little rats some biscuits yesterday and they still came back asking for money."

"Well, let them have it. I've got a purse full of coins I'm never going to figure the value of." She clawed about in her purse before throwing a fistful of change at the pavement. The street kids' reactions were fast, predictable and violent.

"Maddy, look, that's a little girl fighting, look at her go." They swayed off to a waiting taxi and got in without bargaining. The porters and taxi drivers had to break up one particularly violent fist fight. The boy didn't resist as he was dragged away but kept his eyes locked on his enemy, his sister, waiting for the chance to get torn into her again.

The Americans appeared, chubby and jolly, waddling down the stairs, two friendly, clumsy giants. They had been doing good work or God's work and were now going home for Christmas. The terror that the police were going to track me down because of the film on my camera, the faces of Malpas and the street children, and the games that we played with the orphans faded into the past. It was daytime and the taxi drivers, after trying to sell us safaris and tours of the city, came to understand that we were departing. Mike beat them down to 400 shillings easily. There was no victory in this.

Chapter Nine

The bus to Mombasa was hot and uncomfortable. This was to be expected on an eight hour journey along the equator, but we made it hard on ourselves. I had invited the Americans under the misapprehension that they were a couple, yet in fact they had met by accident and were quickly finding out they had nothing in common. The girl, who would have been pretty if she lost a few stone, was some religious freak.

"Sweet Jesus, the things I saw in the Kibera slum. I hope I never have to see or smell poverty like that again. No running water, rotting garbage, girls selling themselves for a dollar. People that couldn't read a bible even if they'd owned one. My church group worked hard there. Now at least some of those slum dwellers will be a light in the eyes of the Lord."

The boy smirked at me and whispered, "The bitches are the thing. Man I can't wait to get with some little honey in Mombasa. They're famous for it down there."

"How did you two meet?"

"I saw a poster about some American barbecue and went down. I should have been suspicious when I saw there wasn't any drink but it was when I heard that music, you know the type that tricks you into thinking it's the Beach Boys and then starts singing about Jesus."

"I see," said Kirsten.

"A beer?" the boy asked.

"Why not? It's Mike's birthday, twenty years old today."

"Well, happy birthday Mikey, grab yourself a can, don't be shy. Say, are you two married?"

We hesitated for a moment and Kirsten changed the hand

she was holding her beer can with before saying, "Yes."

"Cool," the boy said, "cool. I'll probably get married one day too." He drank to that before saying, "I like your accent. Irish isn't it? I wish I had an accent."

"Well you do. I mean you've got an American accent."

"But I mean a real accent like yours."

I hadn't drunk beer for months but I was excited that we were moving one step closer to being home. Usually I didn't take time off for my birthday or Christmas, figuring that it was training on days like those that would give me an advantage over my competitors. But today, with the long journey before us, was pretty much a write-off. Inevitably the beer went straight to my head, and after three cans we were daring each other to ask the driver if he would pull over for a piss stop. But this driver was wearing full bus driver regalia including pristine white gloves and a shirt with lapels. These alone were enough to convince me that this was a man who would not take to interruptions kindly. Not even Kirsten, usually so happy to confront authority figures, was up for this challenge. So we bumped along that road, suffering, not entirely in silence. The Christian girl was fine. She slept and snored loudly.

Eventually we stopped at the Kenyan equivalent of a service station. I went behind some wizened bushes to pee and there got talking to Chad. He had been out working for the Peace Corps for a year.

"Do people still do that? I thought that only happened in the Sixties."

"Sure we do. We have a saying in the Peace Corps," he slurped from his can while buttoning his trousers with one hand, "that a man comes back from Europe cultured, South America a revolutionary, Asia enlightened and Africa an alcoholic." He finished his drink and burped.

There was a small bar at the side of the lay-by and Chad challenged me to see if we could complete a game of pool before the bus left. Considering the state he was in I doubted it, but the table had such a ridiculous slant towards the bottom left pocket that we cleared up in no time.

"That beer had no effect at all," observed Chad cheerfully.

A little old Kenyan man with a white beard and rotten stumpy teeth had been watching us. "This village," he waved his hand, "was born when they found water in an extinct volcano. Now the water has dried up and the village has gone."

"Well ain't that the truth, there's fuck-all here old timer. Say Mike, get this guy a beer."

The old guy repeated his line like a child trying to memorise his part in a school play, working out how to say it to create the best effect. I brought him a beer and as we returned to the bus he held it aloft, toasting us. The journey continued through the massive Tsavo national park. As the sun was setting Kirsten started claiming she could see all sorts of animals, and Chad giggled drunkenly. I started to get a horrible, prickly sweat and felt one of those dehydration headaches kicking in. The old man's line kept rattling about in my head: "The village was born when they found water in an extinct volcano. Now the water has dried up and the village has gone." I searched through my bag but couldn't find a pen. It seemed important that I write it down. Not just the sentiment but the way he had said it. I tried to commit it to memory through repetition.

Mombasa, according to my guidebook, had centuries of history as a major Islamic trading port that was then taken over by the Portuguese in the 16th century. This made it sound as if there'd be sights worth seeing but driving to the centre it just seemed as chaotic and filthy as any other Kenyan city. The bus jerked and jostled along a grand avenue with huge plastic tusks curving over the road. We managed to lose the Americans when collecting our bags, and after the typical tedious negotiations with a taxi driver made our way to the strip of Tourist Hotels on the beach area north of the city.

"The sea should be over there," Kirsten pointed out her window at the dark. "How crazy is it that tomorrow we are going to see the sea and the next day we're going home?"

"A good thing too. I've only got enough antiseptic gel to last another day and I'm totally out of hand wipes."

Our hotel's reception had a thatched roof and wattled walls that were meant to look traditional. The main building behind this looked like any beach hotel in the world. As we waited for our keys we were given two huge cocktails served inside carved-out pineapples. Even the security was kitted out in Maasai costumes and instead of guns carried spears, the only authentic looking things in the place.

We were just in time for the end of dinner – an enormous buffet table filled with half-eaten dishes containing curries, chips, pastas, stroganoffs, and quiches. I piled two plates high, mashing national cuisines into each other. There weren't many guests left eating and I was afraid that the waiters would start taking the food away. Kirsten went for a salad and sat nibbling on a piece of lettuce.

"I wonder what'll happen to all this food?" she asked.

"I'll eat it if they give me a chance," I said cramming some curry drenched quiche into my mouth. "Hey, you should eat some more. You're not going to save Africa by starving yourself."

She gave me one of her death stares and changed the subject. "I got an email from your dad this morning."

"Oh, what was it about?"

"Just to send on his birthday greetings and, well, I think he'd appreciate an email."

"That's rich coming from you."

"It's different with me. My mum will pass on whatever I say to my father. Your dad's got no one. Anyway, how have you managed to fall out with him when you're on the other side of the world?"

"We've not fallen out. I just can't take reading his emails. They say nothing to me. They're the sounds of someone waiting to die, his greatest glory his geraniums."

Kirsten tutted, but laughed.

"I get emails from your dad too," I said, just to shock her.

"Well, I should expect so. He's your coach after all."

"They're not all about running. He does ask after you."

She put her fork down and asked, "Does he ask what kind of shape I'm in?"

"Shape?"

"I mean if I'm looking fit, in good condition, thin?"

"Yeah, I suppose, he asks if you're training well, things like that."

She pushed her plate away, hesitated at the jug of mango juice and instead opened a bottle of water. "What about you and me, does he ask how we're getting on?"

"Once or twice."

"And what do you say?"

"I tell him we're getting along just fine." I said attempting and failing to do a grand American voice.

"Fine?" she said and picked up a dessert spoon. She looked first at her reflection in the concave side then in the convex. "Fine," she said to the spoon. "Why do you think he wanted you to come to Kenya with me? I mean I could have taken anyone but he insisted on you, why was that?"

There were many reasons I thought Mr Harrison had wanted me on this trip. The most important ones were that he wanted someone sensible who knew how to look after himself and would keep an eye on his daughter. After having coached me for four years he could also be certain that I would seize this opportunity with both hands and in doing so compel and cajole Kirsten to train as hard as possible. But these weren't things I could tell Kirsten so I said, "He probably thought we would make a good team."

Kirsten snorted at this and turned the spoon once more to look at her reflection on the other side. "A good team? We're not footballers."

"You know what I mean. Besides, who else could you take? All the girls you used to run with gave up training years ago."

She spun the spoon between her two hands. "Do you remember that training group? Mr Harrison's girls, that's what they used to call us. I was so jealous because I was Mr Harrison's girl. I was his daughter."

"Did you not get a 1-2-3 at the national Cross Country and then clean up all the distance medals on the track one year? What age group were you Under 15s, Under 13s?"

"Under 13 probably, it all started to go wrong once we got a bit older."

She didn't elaborate so I started babbling. "What we all remembered was that from a distance all six of you looked more or less the same. You all seemed to have blonde hair in buns with blue and white hair bands to match the club colours. The boys group used to knock seconds off our split times whenever you lot trained on the track in the hope that you'd notice us. That was when I became a good runner, to be honest. So I had Mr Harrison to thank even then."

She pressed the back of the spoon hard against her forehead. In the other room men with bongo drums and girls dressed in risqué traditional garb were getting ready for a show.

"My dad has some funny ideas about how to get the best out of people. Up until we were 12 or 13 it was alright but there was this one girl, Erin, do you remember her?"

"Erin, yeah, everyone remembers Erin."

"And why's that?"

"Well, she had a great personality."

"You mean she had a great pair of tits, especially at the age when boys started noticing those things."

"It wasn't just that."

"Erin was much better than me when we started Secondary. I don't think I beat her once. But suddenly I started getting closer at training and then in races. By the time we were in third year I didn't even consider her as part of the competition. A great pair of tits and massive hips may help in a lot of situations but they're hardly conducive to running a fast 1500 metres."

"She quit, didn't she?"

"Yeah, she quit. But not after years of doing every session we did, my dad shouting at her to 'make sure she didn't give herself a pair of black eyes,' encouraging the rest of us to laugh at her fat arse when she went off first in handicapped sessions, calling her 'an obese hare that all of us lean greyhounds would easily catch.'"

The music started up in the next room. It sounded strangely like something you'd hear in a Bollywood movie. All the other diners had long since moved through and the waiters who had cleared their tables were hovering.

"Running's a sick world. At school being flat-chested was a bad thing, but in a race it was perfect. And because I cared so much about getting all my dad's attention I dreaded turning into Erin Maclavety. I mean you boys might have thought she was hot but I pitied her, I really did. But obviously things were changing, we were changing, you can't fight nature. At least that's what I thought at the time. Then my dad introduced the Miss Piggy T-shirt."

"The one from the Muppets, I remember it."

"And then came the set of scales that he used to weigh us on every week. I can still see those scales. Probably those other girls who were once my friends can as well. Who ever had put on the most weight during that month had to wear the T-shirt. The rest of us were encouraged to stand around them grunting like pigs, saying that we didn't understand—oink—whenever they spoke, that sort of thing. I mean we were teenage girls, it was natural that we were going to develop. Well it got to the point where the Miss Piggy T-shirt wasn't even washed between sessions, so not only were you a fat pig but you were a smelly fat pig,"

This was classic Mr Harrison. He had so many motivational tricks up his sleeve: throwing the meet's worst performer in the water jump after the steeple chase, making us do interval sessions on sand dunes in climbing boots, telling people to run home from events if they had performed badly then driving along in front of them, stopping and starting, the car always just out of reach, the rest of us jeering out of the windows. He was a tough old-school coach, everyone acknowledged that, but he really knew how to get results. 'I'm either going to make you or break you,' was one of the things he often said.

"It wasn't funny," Kirsten hissed. "All of us started wearing ridiculous amounts of perfume to every training session. Jeanie Gillen went through a period of binding her breasts with bandages. If we were getting weighed that night I wouldn't eat or drink all day. But that wasn't enough. When I was 14 I started developing, I started changing into a woman."

I didn't know if I wanted to hear the rest of this but Kirsten was staring at me with the sort of intimacy demanded by the walking wounded.

"So of course I started putting on weight and for the first time I was the one wearing the Miss Piggy T-shirt, still damp from its last wearer. I was still running well, winning practically everything but my dad started looking at me like he hated me. The other girls loved it because of course they always presumed I was the special one, daddy's girl. I put up with it until one night he made me run in a pig's mask. He said that because I had such an upturned nose I didn't really need it and all the girls laughed. After that session we stopped speaking. I refused to train with him, ran the first half of races so I was well in the lead then walked off the track. He persevered with a couple of the other girls, used to cheer them on instead of me. Even then I think he knew what he was doing, that it was all part of a plan to motivate me to better things."

Of course everyone knew there'd been a massive bust-up between the two of them but this was the first I'd heard of the details. Knowing Mr Harrison I presumed he was only trying to make Kirsten into an even better runner. I looked at her and imagined our parents meeting us at the airport, their faces shocked by how thin she'd become. I could imagine what my dad, who understands nothing about running, would say to me in the car. And already, if I was being honest, I had made up excuses. I would talk about the simple diet, the hard training, blame diarrhoea and sickness. She looked at me and it was clear I was meant to say something sympathetic.

"You're not fat," was the best I came up with.

"I know I'm not fucking fat. All your fucking friends at school used to call me Skeletor. I'm almost 6 foot and right now I'm down to 7 stone 2."

I didn't question how she knew this when she had refused to weigh herself whenever I had asked at the Ks'. Instead I said, "Your nose, it's more like a pixie than a pig."

She burst into laughter, which wasn't the effect I was hoping for, "Oh, you're a charmer. Which brings us back to the question: why would a man like that, a man who wants his daughter never to become a woman, want a boy like you to accompany me round Kenya for three months? Now maybe it's just me but I don't think it's because we make a 'great team.' Now probably it's so he has someone loyal to spy on me – but you're not just that."

"Well what am I?"

"I would say he either thinks you're gay, which is perfect, a chaperone, no threat to his little girl. The other more interesting possibility is that he thinks you're in love with me. That he thinks you'll train really hard to impress me. That he's fucking with you too. Of course if that was the situation he'd have to be pretty sure that I wasn't interested in you. I can't imagine what the two of us getting together would do to him."

She stared at me, her crazy dark eyes, and her haunted, hollow face. I was always useless at knowing if she was meddling or mental. She held my gaze until the head waiter asked us to go because they really needed to clear the room. Next door three middle aged male tourists who were presumably inebriated but possibly just uncoordinated had got up to dance with the Kenyan girls. In some small part of their minds this had probably seemed like a great idea as they swaggered, casting backward grins to their friends, onto the stage. Even from this distance however it looked embarrassing for all. Except perhaps the Kenyan girls, who continued to dance in unison, hidden in their fantastic costumes, looking like they actually enjoyed being on stage: that was certainly no longer the case with the stumbling shoulder shuffling tourists.

"So what's it to be?" Kirsten asked.

I didn't understand the question so said, "Let's get out of here."

Not knowing our way around the hotel we ended up out the back, walking round the swimming pool. A group of mixed nationalities, all about our age, were having a fun time, their eyes gleaming with laughter, their skin burnished by the sun. How happy I would have been to sit with them and go through the motions of a getting-to-know-you conversation. But they looked shocked by the foul expressions on our faces and stopped speaking until we were a safe distance away. The swimming pool area dropped down onto the beach. Kirsten said, "Jambo," to a guard who was being asked to pose for photos with two middle-aged women, one of whom was trying to persuade him to give her his spear. "Can we go down here?"

"Jambo," he replied, "be carefully on the beach."

The bright lights of the hotels along the front glittered gold; their reflection reached out to hold hands across the slick black sea. Even in that dim light it was clear that the sand was of the glaringly white variety beloved of resort brochure front covers. We took our shoes off and walked in it. The top surface had cooled but our feet sank to where the warmth of the day was secreted.

"Why would anyone want to sit round a hotel pool when they have this next to them?"

"Sharks," I replied, "or jellyfish or water pollution."

"Sounds great," said Kirsten sarcastically.

We walked along in a silence more contemplative than content. Two black girls with shiny dresses and friendly smiles appeared out of the darkness. Both carried high heeled shoes. They looked more prepared for a cocktail party than a stroll on the beach.

"Hey," one of them said.

"Hey," I replied.

"Want some company?"

"He's already got company," Kirsten replied. The girls shrugged and peeled off down the beach to walk with their feet in the surf.

"They seemed nice girls, why did you have to be so rude to them?"

Kirsten made a noise that sounded somewhere between a guffaw and someone blowing their nose. "When Moses warned you to be aware of the tigers in Mombasa, what did you think he meant?"

"Oh, I see, so those girls were . . . but they're so young and well dressed."

Kirsten put her arm around my shoulder and said, "Sometimes I wonder if you're for real."

We seemed to be friends again. To celebrate I stooped to pick up a stone that I hoped to skim across the glittering sheen of the sea. But this beach didn't do skimming stones. Or perhaps it did but thousands of boys before me had passed that way with thousands of girls, a feeling of elation welling up in their chests that they only knew how to express, could only perfectly express, by skimming a flat stone across the calm water.

This thought cheered me, as did the hypnotic bass and cross drumming of some reggae rustling through the muffling air. I normally hate reggae, but on a sticky African night by the sea it seemed to be the only music that made sense. Kirsten was already heading in the club's direction so naturally I followed. The place was more of a shack than a bar, lit with fairy lights and candles and half filled by a sound system. They were playing a track full of all the crackly campfire goodness of old vinyl. Kirsten would probably have known who it was but I never asked her. Now in a land smothered by snow and with her long gone I wish that I had. I would do a great deal to hear that song again, to be there in those few minutes again, safe, drunk, sure that we were going home in one piece. Mainly it was just a man singing the line, "I'm still in love with you girl," over and over again. Sometimes I sing it to people but I've forgotten the tune or they've never heard of such a song and they look at me as if I'm crazy.

I sipped the Tusker placed in front of me, not even caring about the diseases I could pick up from the bottle. For the first time in my life I really wanted to dance. I might even have said something about this to Kirsten but for once it was her sitting in a bar looking uneasy, twisting and turning in her seat as if she expected to recognise someone.

A Kenyan girl with a big bubble butt brushed past me on her way to the bar, resting her hand momentarily on my shoulder. She was wearing jeans so tight it seemed they might split at the seams. She leaned at the bar and placed an order, her arse wiggling rhythmically as she put her weight first on one high heeled shoe then the other. Whilst I was spectating, a white man with carved sharp features, dirty blonde hair and a wispy beard had sat next to Kirsten. They seemed to be having a very intense conversation. I was about to intervene but Kirsten looked up at me as if she was having trouble recognising my face. The chubby Kenyan girl continued swaying to the music.

The man talking to Kirsten was wearing ripped up shark attack chic clothes that looked very cheap but had probably cost him a great deal. He was about thirty and had that world-weary look, somewhere between a troubadour and a travelling salesman. "I like your earrings," I heard him saying. "They're very ethnic."

"What does that even mean? Everything's ethnic," I said, but he didn't seem to hear me.

"This is Joey," shouted Kirsten. "He's travelled right across Africa. From the Congo to Kenya."

"That must be a logistical nightmare."

"It wasn't easy," he replied, with a look that said I'd have no idea how difficult it actually was. "But I was embedded with

142

some Charities for much of the way, taking photographs so that they have evidence of all the good work they are doing. They helped organise things."

There was no way I was going to compete with that and I found myself asking, "Did you get any good pictures?"

"Thousands I think, I'm up for three awards in January. But I'm not so sure I know what a good picture is anymore. I took a series of a man being executed near the border between Zaire and Rwanda. The execution was going to take place whether I took the photos or not, so I thought, 'Why not capture it? Freeze this moment between life and death. Only a photo can do that, right?' But the look on that man's face as he stood there waiting to be shot . . ." The photographer shook his head, picked up his beer bottle to drink, put it down then lifted it again, shaking it to once and for all confirm it was finished. He had a strange accent. South African or Dutch I thought. For some reason I didn't trust him.

"But is there not a feeling amongst photographers that you've got some sort of right, I mean responsibility to bear witness?"

The man took out some skins and rolling tobacco, which he worked with while answering. "Yes, but to what end? I take the photo, win a prize, have an exhibition, make money from others' suffering. People come and see it and tell me these are great photos, that they are moved. But how moved? Are they going to give up their homes and family to devote their life to fighting injustices? Would they even notice the executed man if he cleaned their streets or poured their coffee? No, of course not. They look at the photos and have had their dose of suffering for the day. They've sympathised, probably imagined they've empathised and they think this is enough. If the man was pouring their coffee it would be more difficult, but with these photos they can tell themselves, I didn't shoot that man, I didn't stop the rains that caused the famine."

"But if they donate some money or one person starts campaigning against the arms trade then your photos have achieved something. Is that not enough?" asked Kirsten.

"I don't know if any response is enough."

"But didn't you take any positive photos? I mean there's lots to despair about but we've seen projects that bring hope, played with children who were happy."

"I take some but it is not what the aid agencies want. It's not what I want." He lit the rollie and inhaled hard. "Horror and sadness sell, horror and sadness make people reach in their pocket and donate." He sounded irritated by my last question. "If only you'd seen that man's face before he was executed. The whole series of photos. One critic said they reminded him of Holbein or Grunewald and their 'grotesque depictions of Christ.' That's what I want. Images that make people guilty, that stop them eating, that make them never want to spend money on make-up or clothes or alcohol ever again. Every day thousands of Africans die for our sins." He tapped ash from the smouldering end of his rollie into an empty beer bottle. "I want to rub the West's nose in this." No-one said anything for a bit. The reggae music continued. In the corner a TV beamed images from the glamorous world of pop videos, where everyone is fashionable and beautiful and arrive in limousines. Below this the Kenyans danced, laughed and hugged each other. Every once in a while one of them looked up at the TV, a shadow of doubt flickering across their face.

"More drinks?" I suggested. Joey indicated that the bottles were empty by way of saying this was a good idea. The bar was crowded and I felt bounced between bums as I waited. There is apparently an optimum leaning angle that attracts a barman's attention without seeming too aggressive but if such a thing existed I never mastered it. Instead I thought of questions to ask the photographer, questions that would make me sound knowledgeable and him less heroic. After about ten minutes I was served and returned to our table, which was now occupied by a group of Kenyan men. I stood about for a couple of minutes drinking my beer too quickly and no longer wishing to dance.

This was the Kitun Cave and the club in Eldoret all over again. Her getting in trouble through going off somewhere dangerous while expecting me to follow. I wanted to let her be, sort out her own mess; I ended up on the beach calling her name. If I caught them coupling, unaware, I didn't know if I would kill him or watch. But no-one answered apart from the two girls we had met on the beach before. Every time I shouted: "Kirsten!" they replied "How-wah-yooo?"

I decided to walk back to the hotel along the main road, thinking that being among bright lights and people might be safer, and hoping that I might catch up with them and somehow intervene. I cursed Kirsten for her stupidity and doubted that Joey, if that was his real name, was even a photographer. There was something about Kirsten that attracted the type of man who would tell her stories of suffering and sadness, looking into her hollow eyes and knowing she would provide a sympathetic ear, a rub of the head, a squeeze of the shoulder.

There had been an accident on the road and traffic was tailed back in both directions. People were climbing out of their cars, shouting to those further up the road for information. The place reeked of exhaust fumes and the stench of burnt rubber. A Matatu bearing the slogan, 'The Road's Going to Burn' on its sliding doors had crashed head on into a farm truck bringing chickens into the city markets. The resulting mess of glass and feathers, runaway animals and injured passengers was attracting quite a crowd. I walked past trying not to look, feeling ghostlike as the only white person: for once not attracting any attention. About 100 metres from the crash I saw electric blue neon lights saying *The Paradise Nightclub*. Remembering Jeremiah saying that this was the place I should go if I really wanted to celebrate my birthday, I turned off the road.

The track to the club was bordered by thick dark-leaved bushes that gave off a sweet, clammy smell. Two girls standing near these called out, "Jambo," as if they had been waiting for me all their lives. I returned the greeting and, mustering some of the words the iron men had taught me, said, "Habari gani?"

The girls giggled and clapped. "Nzuri," the one with a red sequined dress and matching hair band replied. She took my left arm and the other girl, who was almost as tall as me and very elegant, took my right. The club had the same sort of faux-thatched roof as the entrance to our hotel; there was a couple of bouncers wearing what looked like Coldstream Guard uniforms, minus the big furry helmets. I checked that my wallet was still in my pocket and allowed myself to be led in.

"It's my birthday," I told the taller girl.

"It most certainly is," the other replied.

I felt a bit of a star strolling into that place with a girl on either arm. *If only Kirsten could see me now* was one thought that rollicked drunkenly through my mind. A wooden dance floor and a ruffled curtain hiding a small cabaret stage were illuminated by red spotlights, while the rest of the place was shadowy, dark wooden features everywhere. I would have waited a couple of seconds for my eyes to adjust if I was on my own, but the girls knew where we were going. The patrons, all men, white, Arabic or from the Far East, sat in small semi-circular booths facing the dance floor. Each table had at least two or three Kenyan girls, pawing the men and pouring their drinks.

The girl with the red dress led me by the hand to our table. As we sat, a man wearing a Hawaiian shirt so hideous that I immediately thought he must be the proprietor came and spoke to us.

"Enjoy your own slice of the magnificent gateau that is Africa." He patted his paunch like it was a bum bag containing something valuable, and smiled at me. There were suds of beer in the hairs of his wispy moustache and his face was a landslide of blotchy skin and blown blood vessels. A real booze hound by the looks of things but there was something there underneath the alcoholic mask that I thought I recognised.

"I'm sorry honey, I have to go but I leave you in Mercy's capable hands."

The tall girl gave me a nervous smile. She had long straightened hair and lips sticky as sucky sweets.

"My grandmother's name was Mercy," I stupidly told her. "But she's dead now." This comment must have made me look so despondent that the girl took pity on me.

"My name's not really Mercy, it's Hannah, but we aren't meant to tell clients our real names here."

"Oh ok. Hannah's a nice name," I had an obese drooling aunt called Hannah but I had learnt my lesson by then. Mercy and Hannah, though: I'd never met any prostitutes before but they didn't have names like that in the films I'd seen.

"Maybe we should have a drink," Hannah suggested. Almost immediately a waiter in waistcoat, white shirt and bow tie appeared.

"Sir?"

"A vodka tonic."

"And the lady?"

"A gin and tonic."

He nodded and turned smartly on his heel.

The drinks cost about twenty times more than the round I'd bought in the reggae place. The girl leaned into me, her bare shoulder touching my bicep. She smelt faintly of singed hair and coconuts.

"So is it really your birthday?"

"Yep, I'm twenty today."

"Really, I'm twenty as well," Hannah said, as if she'd just discovered we had a mutual friend in China or twelve webbed toes each. She fluttered heavy fake lashes at me; the makeup on her eyelids was a sparkly blue.

"Where are you from?" She asked.

"Scotland."

"Scotland," she exclaimed like someone auditioning for a bad play, "Do you know why all the women in the world love the Scottish man?"

There didn't seem to be any obvious answer to this so I

admitted that I did not.

"It is because of Sean Connery." She smiled uncertainly. "Sean Connery is Scottish?"

"Yes."

"Oh good." She fiddled with the strap on her shoe and admitted, "They get us to learn lines like that. I've memorised the names of actors and pop stars from about 30 different countries. The Japanese ones are the hardest."

I felt confused about why she was telling me this.

"I'm sorry Maria had to go." She nodded at the girl in the red sparkly dress who was now on the dance floor. "I could get you another girl, we even have some Russian girls," she said quite proudly.

"Don't worry about it," I replied but she was waving over a wiry blonde girl with glaringly white skin who somehow negotiated her way between tables, despite wearing massive sunglasses.

"Who's the man in the Hawaiian shirt?"

"That's Jeff, he runs his place. He's from Holland but he's been here forever."

Suddenly I made the connection. "Has he got a son, Joey, a photographer?"

"He's got a son called Joey, sure, but he's more a philanderer than a photographer." I laughed at this and the girl laughed too. "He's just a beach bum really. I think he used to be a professional photographer but he said the whole thing fatigued him. That's the word he used. Let me tell you about fatigue I had wanted to say. Now he spends all his time drinking and trying to pick up tourists. We girls in here aren't good enough for him."

"Your English is pretty amazing. Did you learn it from—" and here I didn't want to say customers or clients so after some thought settled on, "—tourists?"

"No. I'm a university student in my third year. You need to be good at English to get that far."

I figured this was just another of the lines they learnt to

impress customers, but didn't get to ask her any more as the Russian girl came and perched next to me. She crossed her legs with a rustle of complicated underthings and flattened a black Tutu, so that she was sitting comfortably. "Hi, I'm Svetlana, I'm a professional dancer," she said, looking at Hannah in a superior fashion.

"Pleased to meet you."

The girl pouted duck lips at me and said, "Want to dance?"

At this point they were playing some terrible music from the mid-nineties, Coronna—*This Is The Rhythm Of The Night*, I seem to remember. Slinky slim slips of Kenyan girls were dancing about, all bangles and hair sprayed curls. A fat middle-aged European man shambled about on the spot hardly able to stop his tongue from hanging out. Above them all a giant disco ball rotated ineffectually, the light that should have reflected off its thousand square mirrors broken. "I'm not really much of a dancer."

"As you please." The girl said, scraping hair white as an old lady's back into a ballerina bob. The sunglasses partially hid acne scars on her cheek, but I kept looking at them. I had a feeling that there was something strange about her eyes that she didn't want people to see. She sat with the poise of a concert violinist, tendons working on her neck as she made bitchy comments about the people bobbing about on the dance floor.

I stirred the ice in my glass and sucked up some watery vodka. The waiter appeared the moment I had put my glass down and we ordered two more drinks. "So how did you end up here?" I asked.

"It's a long story." She made a throwing away a piece of litter gesture. "I tell you later, but I need more drinks in me first."

"And are there other girls from Russia working here?"

"Oh, yes, I am having one other Russian friend and another from Romania. The customers from the Middle East and Japan are liking us best. Most westerners are happy with the Kenyan girl. I guess everyone is after the exotic."

Looking at the two girls I understood what she meant. Svetlana, when she wasn't speaking in that deep Russian voice, could easily be from Scotland. She was the prettier of the two, more natural and flirty. It wasn't hard to imagine fucking her. But Hannah was different, not just foreign but distant. There was a shy and defiant look in her big watery eyes: it said I could speak, drink, sleep with her but I wouldn't know her real thoughts, her feelings or her name. This was a big turn on, the idea that there was something that she was unwilling to give, something that wasn't up for sale.

As if reading my thoughts Svetlana tried to retrieve the situation. "And you, why are you in Mombasa?"

"I'm on my way home from an athletic training camp in the Rift Valley."

"So you're a famous runner," she said squeezing my quadriceps.

"Yes," I replied, liking the sound of it.

"How many days are you here?" asked Hannah, who had been delicately fondling her glass and sipping on her straw.

"We leave the day after tomorrow."

"Then you have time to see Fort Jesus and swim in the reef."

"And the crocodile farm," added Svetlana.

"I'm not swimming in any crocodile farm."

"The crocodile farm is not important, it is only for stupid tourists," insisted Hannah.

"I like going there," Svetlana continued, looking at a group of Arabs wearing scarves and dishdashas who had just entered; they were looking around the place as if they owned it. "The crocodile farm is a sad place. Most of the animals are kept only for their meat. The crocodiles on show are the freak ones, albinos, Siamese twins, animals that would never survive in the wild."

The Arabs had been consulting with Hawaiian-shirted Jeff, who pointed over to our table. Svetlana ignored them and continued. "The only normal crocodile on show is this giant called Albert. He ate three Zambians apparently. They've given him an enclosure with a pool and everything. He's the zoo celebrity."

"And the farmed crocodiles?"

"They're kept in these walled off pits. You're not meant to see them. Maybe you should take a peek tomorrow. You don't mind paying for this?" She asked as another drink was delivered.

"So, what will I see?"

"Many crocodiles crawling about one on top of the other in the dark." She wrinkled her nose at me, then scanned the bar. "And who would want to eat crocodile meat anyway?"

"You don't think it's natural?"

"No, I don't," she replied, picking up her handbag and swooshing her Tutu up behind her. "Enjoy your evening." She took the straw and paper parasol from the glass and downed her drink. The Arabs welcomed her to their table and she snuggled in amongst them, already making eyes at a waiter.

"She has quite an aptitude for alcohol," said Hannah in admiration. I watched her long fingers and pale palms play with her glass. "I, on the other hand, dislike to be inebriated." She smiled, showing a string of white teeth. There was something about this girl with her awkwardness, her grand vocabulary and her RP voice. Sitting next to her I felt as if a small animal that had been hibernating in the pit of my stomach was suddenly stirring again.

"Well, why don't we stop drinking and go somewhere else?" I didn't really know what I was proposing, the words just came out. "I don't really feel like I belong here."

Hannah looked a little perplexed before saying, "No, I don't either."

Brilliant, I thought, I've pulled. Admittedly anyone with a few thousand shillings in their pocket would have been as successful, but at the time I felt like an all-conquering hero. I told myself all the usual stories, that Hannah was actually a waitress and this was a one-off, that she didn't need the money.

All night long I looked for signs that she was relieved it was me and not some fat old man with weird perversions.

We left the place to the sound of Ride on Time by Black Box and the sight of Arabs in dishdashas, Japanese in suits and Westerners in Hawaiian shirts and khaki shorts dancing with scantily clad Kenyans, all sweating under the sultry red spot lights and the enormous disco ball that didn't sparkle.

Once we were out on the main road I was unsure what to do, but Hannah clung to my arm, leading the way. The smashed up Matatu and Farm truck had been pushed to the side of the road and the few late night vehicles zipped along the road at their usual suicide pace.

"My hotel's just a couple of hundred metres from here."

"Where are you staying?"

"The Reef."

"That's a nice hotel but I'm afraid they won't let me in there."

"But I've paid for a double room, I'm sure if I explained . . ."

She shook her head. "They know me there," was all she said. "There's a place down here that's more accommodating."

There was something about her professionally brisk way of talking that chilled me on that sweaty night, even with her damp smooth arm pressed against mine.

"So, have you only just started working at the club?" I asked, full of hope.

"No, I've been working a couple of nights a week for almost two years now." I started making unpleasant calculations in my head. "It's an interesting set up. Girls like me pay to escort men to the club but once we're there we get a commission on all the drinks you buy. As you saw, I'm not much of a drinker, but there are plant pots and umbrella buckets all over the place. It's a lucky thing all the plants are plastic as they wouldn't grow so straight and that's no lie. If we want to make any extra money, well that's our business."

We cut down an unlit path, the asphalt under our feet changing to sand. There, hidden amongst the palm trees and between two towering hotels, was a small ramshackle bungalow.

A backpacker couple sat on the porch smoking. I was too embarrassed to look at them but they were oblivious to me. The receptionist, a small Kenyan with shirt buttoned to the neck and tightly knotted tie, was drinking whisky.

"Welcome," he cried. "Double room, short stay."

Hannah didn't even answer him, just picked up a pen to scribble a name in the ledger. "It's 1000 shillings."

I scrabbled in my wallet looking for the correct note but also making sure I had my trusty condom. There he was, the yellow scratched off the pack in places to reveal the tinfoil silver. I checked the 'best before' date. Above the reception hung an electric fly killer. Every few seconds there was a crackle like a bulb blowing. I flinched every time I heard it but the other two acted like it wasn't even there. After I had paid the receptionist said, "Name?"

I picked up the pen and wrote, *Sebastian Coe*. The girl had a quick squint at it then back at me, squeezing her eyes as if trying to remember something. As we walked along the corridor she said, "I cost 3000 shillings for a short stay."

This was about 25 pounds. I wasn't going to start haggling at this stage but I guessed she was ripping me off. Had Jeremiah not said that old clapped out prostitutes could be bought in Eldoret for 20 shillings? Not that I'd thought for one moment of going there. Hannah was young and beautiful and not knocking on death's door: not yet anyway.

Our room smelt of disinfectant and boiled cabbage, the plaster walls were wet and the door wouldn't lock properly. My heart fluttered like an autumn leaf as she turned to face me; she looked young and uncertain now that we were alone in a room together.

"What do you do again?" she asked me.

"I don't know, I thought you were the expert."

"Sorry no, I meant as a job, are you a famous runner or something? I thought I recognised your name?"

"No, that wasn't my real name. I'm Mike, I study Sports Science."

"Really, I'm majoring in human biology."

"So you're actually a student?"

"Yes." She pouted petulantly to show my disbelief had hurt her. "This semester we've mostly been looking at Gross Anatomy and Ethical Foundations. What about you?"

"I've been doing research on various physical responses elite athletes experience when changing altitude."

So we sat on the corner of the bed discussing biology until she excused herself and said, "I need to pee."

The wooden bathroom door had become warped with all the damp, and ground against the floor as she tried to wedge it shut. I lay back on the prickly army issue type blanket and watched two mosquitoes jigging around the naked light. She had turned the taps on so I wouldn't have to hear her piss. It was one, two in the morning, something like that. It suddenly seemed important that I got some sleep, but the click of her heels told me she had returned to the room, and I felt the mattress dip as she crawled onto the bed beside me. Her shoes clattered to the floor and she whispered, "Mike."

Should I have pretended to be asleep? She unbuttoned my shirt and her nails trailed across my stomach before unbuckling my belt. There was no chance I was getting to pretend I was asleep now, not even if I had wanted to.

She took my cock in her mouth and started sucking. It wasn't like it needed any encouragement. I squeezed my eyes shut and felt my thigh and stomach muscles tense. It felt like she had taken the whole of my penis in her mouth. I opened my eyes to see if this was even possible but a veil of her long straightened hair tickling across my navel prevented me from seeing. As if sensing this, her head rose and she flicked her hair round to the other side of her head, looked me right in the eye and went down again. My buttocks clenched and I tried to think of Dot Cotton, the 7 times table, but it was no good. I pulled away from her mouth and spurted all over her face.

"Hey!" she said looking at me with the unstuck eye.

"Sorry," I stuttered.

"Have you been saving up for this all week?"

"I've been saving up for this all my life," I corrected her.

She unpeeled the congealed fake eyelash and wiped some of the semen from her cheek. "Well, I can't go back to the club looking like this." She tossed the fake eyelashes on the bedside table and looked at me like something out of *A Clockwork Orange*.

"Well, maybe we can try again."

"Sure, you're the one that's paying." I was back to looking at the ceiling, only this time with my limp cock sticky with saliva and curled up like a slug when you pour salt on it. Hannah went to the toilet to clean my cum off her face. The whole situation was very unsatisfactory.

She sang, hummed, whistled a tune, a whole orchestra in her head coming in with their own parts: a timpani of falling water. I watched as she came back into the room with her top off – as I had made a mess of it – white bra beautiful against her dark breasts. She was much shorter, less predatory without the heels; her face was blurry, softer without all the makeup. I felt the first twitching of desire and knew the night was not lost.

She curled up on the bed next to me and I rolled over to face her and reached out to place my hand on the dip between her hip and rib cage. Her skin was remarkably smooth and warm, like someone who has just come in from lying in the sun. I reached round and unbuttoned her bra, one-handed, first time! She wriggled out of her bra. Her breasts were paler than the rest of her skin. They were quite small but the nipples were really big. Did this mean she'd had children? I knew everything about biology but nothing about breasts.

I reached out and touched them, the way a child as a dare might touch a beached jellyfish. My fingers were sweaty and I thought she wouldn't like these clammy hands squeezing her. She put a hand behind her back, unclipped and unzipped herself and raised her hips to pull her skirt down. I took off my shirt and trousers, relieved that she hadn't removed her panties. This was actually going to happen; nothing was going to stop it. I ran my hand up the inside of her thigh and she moved her legs slightly apart.

"One moment," she said, and reached over to her handbag.

Realising what she was doing I said, "It's alright, I've got one," and retrieved the condom that had waited patiently, heavy as a debt, in my wallet. Trying to open the foil packet with my sweaty hands I thought for the first time about HIV and what risks I was taking, but there was no stopping me now. She had removed her panties and after a struggle I managed to unroll the condom. Was it inside out? I wasn't sure. I rolled over on top of her. She opened her legs, spat on her fingers and rubbed herself. I glanced down at her chubby black thighs, groomed prickly hair and entered her. She made a noise like a polite cough and I started thrusting, slowly at first, fascinated by her face, eyes half closed, lips half opened. She hooked her heels round the back of my calf muscles. I took in her smell of singed hair and coconut. I continued battering away, staring at her face, searching for a flicker of response. She looked to the side, her breathing ragged, nostrils flaring. She kept lifting her hands about to grip my back then letting them fall to make bunches in the bed sheets. I came with a shout and buried my head in her hair, breathing in her smells and shuddering.

I lay like that until my breathing was back to normal and my heart had stopped ricocheting about in my chest. As I withdrew the condom came off – unless it had come off earlier. It lay on the bed like some deceased deep water animal waiting for examination. My milky cum filled the teat, smudges of what I guessed was menstrual blood smeared the rubber. And then that ridiculous sickly strawberry smell like a fresh packet of bubblegum. She took a tissue from her handbag and expertly picked up the offending article, folded it away and threw it in the bin.

She quickly got dressed, turning her back to me. I would

have been happy to lie there, but realised that very soon I would be naked and she would be clothed, so I threw my clothes on.

"That'll be 3000 shillings," she said in a voice that could have got her a job on the reception desk at the Hilton.

"Here, make it 4000," I said, shuffling through the filthy notes I'd never have the time to spend.

"Thanks. If you close the door when leaving, I need to freshen up." She was busy zipping my money into a serious looking wallet. I waited to see if she was joking, if she was going to spare me a smile.

Striding down the corridor I nearly collided with the manager, who said, "That was a long, short stay." If he'd tried to stop me I'd probably have hit him. On the way out I kicked a palm tree and felt my toe crack. I started sprinting home, focusing only on the pain in my foot. I really wanted a shower. Like that could save things. My toe hurt even through my drunkenness and anger, and I realised it'd be bad in the morning. The hotel, with its fake ethnic decorations and frigid air, was just round the corner. I collected my key. The receptionist looked at me, lip-stick smeared and bleary-eyed, shocked white by a few hours under the African night. She had seen it all before.

My room was as untouched as when I'd left it, my suit case unpacked. I opened the sliding door to my small balcony that adjoined Kirsten's. Despite the late hour her lights were on. I leant out over the wall, sick with the thought of what I might see. In a way I wanted it, the worst. If I could get that I knew I could walk down onto the beach, wade out into the sea and swim until the hotels on the shore were a smear of lights and I couldn't go any further. She hadn't shut the blinds, so only these semi-transparent muslin curtains covered the window. But there was no one inside. Maybe she had left it like that when we went out? Then I heard a noise like someone gagging. I immediately thought of the prostitute going down on me. I heard the noise again, unmistakably from her room. I felt nauseated with disgust and excitement at the thought of Kirsten doing something like that. Then I heard her vomiting. This sequence of noises happened a couple of times. Only after it had stopped did I shout, "Kirsten, Kirsten, are you all right?"

There was no reply for about a minute, but then she came onto her balcony. Instead of brushing aside the curtains she walked through them so that they hung over her face like a bridal veil. "Yes."

"I've done something really stupid. Fuck, I think I'm going to die. I'm sure, I can feel it."

"Tell me about it."

"This isn't some melodrama. I've just had sex with a prostitute and think the condom came off.

She pulled the veil over her head. The rims of her eyes were red raw. I remembered a primary school teacher once telling me never to paint eyes with whites around the iris, as only mad people have eyes like this.

"What do you mean the condom came off?"

"I mean it wasn't on . . . at the end."

"Christ, what's that? Playing Russian roulette with one, two bullets in the gun?"

She was rubbing her bare arms even though it was far from cold, and I was shivering and felt my bones would splinter if I didn't sit down. I was acutely aware of the pulse in my wrist, the feeling of something like a ball bearing stuck in my vein.

"I'm sorry, just when you went off with Joey . . . and then these girls showed up and it all happened, like a bad dream, it didn't seem I was making the decisions."

She shook dramatically, wiped her lips and examined the back of her hand. "I didn't go with that guy, not that it helps. I just went home. I was feeling sorry for myself and didn't feel like good company. I'm sorry I left you."

"It's not your fault."

"Should I come round?"

"Please."

So we lay in one bed for a second night, curled tight, arms

tangled together as if we actually protected each other. She slept and I listened to her taking miraculous shallow intakes of air. And when she breathed out, her breath smelt of sour milk. I lay there trying to smother my waking thoughts in a pillow; trying to replace the smell of coconut and singed hair with something closer to home.

Chapter Ten

If you were with me floating in salt water, you would spy a cloud innocent as candy floss, the postcard perfect beach, a Kenyan selling sunglasses and a dhow floating in the background to authenticate the scene. This beach was just crazy beautiful. Everything had gone to fuck but this was still a beautiful beach. If you were with me, we could watch the group of snorkellers not 50 metres away blowing bubbles and startling darts of stunning fish into jumping out of the water. A reef that just broke the surface kept this part of the sea still as a lagoon and I would tell you it protected us from sharks. The water was warm, so salty that if I didn't move a muscle I felt I was levitating. You would tell me we were safe

The shouting of a man carrying a pole tied to which were kaleidoscopic shawls, and another man pushing a trolley loaded with a refrigerated box made me stand up. They bawled the names of their wares even though there were few tourists. Most of the guests couldn't be bothered with the harassment and were spending their day by the pool, beneath the plastic palm leaves, protected by the guards and their spears and the sign that said NO TREESPASSING!

But *man*, the hotel was mobbed with couples on their honeymoons. Hands constantly holding hands, heads constantly tilting as if the experience of being photographed so much at their weddings had made them believe that every moment was a picture opportunity. They would pose on bridges, in sunsets, colourful cocktails in hand, looking for a third person to take the shot, hoping that this wasn't another moment that would only be recorded in the photo album of the mind. I wondered if anyone thought Mike and I were a couple. Too young, too glum, probably.

Waking this morning I had first realised that my breath smelt foul, then that he was in the bed, and I couldn't remember if I was in my room or his. I went to the bathroom and used his toothpaste and some mineral water to freshen my mouth. I watched him sleeping for a while, looking at his muscular sinewy arms, strong clenched face. It seemed ridiculous that his body could carry something that would kill him, but he probably looked at me faking my way through life and thought the same thing.

I blazed back to the beach past the gauntlet of men selling coconuts and paintings of elongated silhouettes walking into African sunsets. I showered off the sea salt, conscious of the bikinied slabs of frying flesh eyeing me like I was some rare kind of animal. Wrapping a towel around my hips, I flung on a shirt that stuck to my damp skin.

I flip-flopped back to the hotel and knocked on Mike's door. He opened, washed and dressed, fresh and fit as normal.

"How you feeling?" I blurted out.

"Not good, not good." He rubbed a bit of imaginary sleep from the corner of his eye. "Bit of a creeping nausea every few minutes and ridiculously weak. I don't think I'll be running anywhere today."

"Well no one's expecting you to." I reached out to rub his upper arm, but at the last moment decided to redesign my shower flattened hair. "Are there any initial symptoms, of, you know?"

"Contracting HIV. I think there's a few," he answered brusquely, "but differentiating them from a hangover would be difficult." He sounded so professional and detached that I started crying. "What are you crying for?" He asked before hugging my wet body, and holding my blubbering face close to his chest. "Listen, I looked in the guidebook. There's a hospital just a couple of miles down the road. I'm going to grab a taxi and get tested. Clear this thing up."

I sniffled. "Are you sure they can just tell you like that?"

"Might need to hang about for a bit, but it'll be a weight off my mind."

"What about needles – I mean, will it be safe?"

"I'll ask the right questions."

"Ok, if you're sure." I dabbed my eyes with the cuff of my shirt, "Hold on two minutes and I'll get changed and come with you."

"No, don't do that." He sounded alarmed. "It's not fair wasting your last day. This is my problem, I'll sort it."

"But really, I don't mind. You can't just go on your own."

"Look at the sunshine, the beach and the sea." He waved out the window. "This is paradise. Enjoy it, you won't be here long." And with that he guided me out the room as if I were a blind person or the Queen and then strode off down the corridor, shouting, "And make sure you have a good lunch."

Alone in my room, I dropped the towel and took off my wet T-shirt. Stark in the mirror were the lines and folds of my half naked self. I stood looking at my reflection for a couple of minutes, running my fingers along my bones. My head looked like it had been superimposed on a child's body. Taut neck tendons looked ready to snap as I encircled the tops of my arms with cold bony fingers. It was lunchtime and even though I hated eating amongst people I made myself go down the stairs. I was so hungry that the pattern in the corridor carpet writhed like a sick thing. *Who needs drugs when you can do this to yourself?* said a horrible little voice in the back of my head.

Before I got to the dining room I spotted a cluster of computers, and decided to Google 'HIV testing.' As usual, the internet was screen-smashingly slow and every guest on their way to lunch could see what I was searching for. Eventually the information came up, confirming what I had expected: an HIV antibody test was a total waste of time and certain results could only be obtained after 3 months.

I raced out the front and jumped in the nearest local taxi. "To the hospital!" I shouted, resisting the urge to ask the driver to step on it.

The journey was short and expensive, but I didn't care about that. There were hundreds of men sitting on the kerb, women wailing in groups, children hurdling and dancing around them. A shoe shiner asked if I wanted my shoes polished which didn't make any sense since I was wearing flip flops. A woman with a stall selling medicinal bottles of what looked like cooking herbs pointed at me and shouted, "I have the solution!" but I knew that she didn't.

Everywhere was that smell of flesh sweating in the sun. An ambulance arrived, its siren lassoing round itself. People stood up and craned their necks. There was a hush as two people were stretchered out and rushed into the hospital on trolleys. I followed them, looking so certain the security guards didn't dare stop me.

Inside was chaos: total, utter chaos. At least a dozen dark shiny faces looked at me, their head wounds puckering, lips burst, noses bleeding. Other men and a couple of women held broken forearms tenderly, their grey faces wincing. A boy no older than 14 stared furiously as doctors and nurses flapped past. His shoulder looked like it was dislocated. "Miss, can you help me?"

"What's happened?"

"There has been a manifestation and the police intervened. Now can you help me?"

I averted my eyes and said, "I'll see what I can do." More people limped in, some held up by friends. All that blood and a smell like baked beans. I walked out the door and threw up. I started striding in the direction of the hotel, not pausing to ask for directions nor daring to look back, afraid that the boy with the dislocated shoulder would come after me and demand that I did something.

I'd been stupid to come chasing after Mike. How did I think

I was going to find him? In fact I doubted he had even come to the hospital. Surely if I suspected an HIV test the day after a possible infection was useless then Mr Science himself would know it for certain. So why would he come here? If he really didn't know that a HIV test at this stage was useless then the doctors at the hospital would tell him. There was nothing for me to do. I mentally scrubbed my hands of the whole affair.

Reaching a big bridge that I hadn't remembered crossing on the journey there I consulted the Lonely Planet's map. I seemed to be going in the right direction and thought I could even see the famous Fort Jesus. I took out Mike's camera hoping the zoom would help me recognise what I was looking at, but the castle or whatever it was stood too far away.

I leaned over the river looking at the choppy brown water. On the concrete supports under the first arc of the bridge lay a dozen or so bodies; their loose limbs and abandoned postures made them look like they had been dropped from a great height. Maybe you think I should have got used to seeing people so dusty and forgotten, got used to the various contorted positions people adopted in a desperate attempt to find comfort where there wasn't any. I took out the camera full of intent. The photographer from last night had started using phrases like "The pornography of suffering." Did that describe this impulse to record and save something? Mike's camera had automatic focus but getting a good shot would be hard because of the change from the sunlight in which I stood to the shadows under the bridge's arc. The bodies remained still. I checked around me, feeling like a spy taking photos of state secrets. Two men with bulging muscles, the sweat running off their skin, pushed a cart laden with bags of charcoal. A couple of cyclists, a Matatu spray-painted with faces of Arsenal players, and a wedding party posing for pictures. I would have liked to have taken photos of all of this, but an old man with milky white eyes and a hideously deformed foot was watching me. He sat on the other side of the bridge, on bundles of newspaper, occasionally rubbing the foot that lay out in the sun for all to see. Not that he could have fitted shoes or socks over the bulbous growths but maybe a blanket or sheet of newspaper would have been decent. A passing woman stopped and they spoke together. He beamed up into her face, smiling like only the visually impaired, the unphotographed, and children know how to smile. She pressed some coins into his hand and continued her journey. He kept up his observation of a point on the bridge just to my right, an inane look of contentment filling his face.

Clearly this man was blind; but it didn't matter, I'd stuffed Mike's camera back in the rucksack, another photo untaken. As I proceeded along the bridge I met a Kenyan wedding party, which was being arranged in all the typical combinations photographers believe make good pictures. The bride was young and shining and beautiful, the groom slightly older but with a handsome, scholarly air. Their appearance and that of their guests suggested they were all from that tiny privileged group of upper class Kenyans. The ubiquitous street kids expecting a few 5 or 10 shilling notes were stopping other pedestrians so that nothing would block the photos. Their industry and the seriousness with which they undertook their task reminded me of Malpas and our luminous shirted gang back in Eldoret. In truth they needn't have bothered, as most people were happy to stand and watch the beautiful clothes, the bride giggling nervously, and the bridesmaids fussing around her white dress trying to keep it out of the dust.

The photographer wore a suit so baggy it was surely borrowed, a sweat drenched trilby worn at a rakish angle, and old shoes polished to within an inch of their life. He fawned, he persuaded, he expressed delight, all the time clicking away like an insect. I had no idea what he'd get paid for this job, but by the looks of him it wasn't much. I thought of the Dutch photographer from last night worrying about his prize money and awards. If this photographer was to wheel round and take photos of those bodies under the bridge or capture the blind leper in the background of a wedding shot, would that not be a photo worth taking? Would he not be able to win awards and get published in magazines as easy as a European or American photographer? Point, focus, click, repeat. Surely that was all there was to it?

Once all the permutations had been exhausted the guests climbed into waiting taxis. A couple of notes were peeled off and given to the biggest of the street boys to be fought over or shared out as he saw fit. I waited in the hope there'd be more taxis than were needed, but they were all taken. It was that moment I spotted Mike. The sight of me seemed to make him stumble, but he adjusted himself and, after a tuck, zip, rub of nose and claw of hair, looked me straight in the eye.

"What are you doing here?" he asked, pretending to be delighted at the surprise meeting.

"I was just on my way to the hospital."

"You walked?"

"Yeah."

"Jesus, why?"

"I wanted to make sure you were all right." He mumbled something and we set off down the road. "Well? Are you?"

"Yeah," he said gruffly, before grinning. "All clear."

He must have seen the look of disbelief on my face because he held up his left arm to show me where a plaster had been stuck over the injection point.

"For real?" I said. "That's terrific news."

"Yeah, I wasn't too worried but it's nice to have it cleared up."

"Of course," I said, feeling weak. "Hold on a sec." I leaned against the bridge's railing fighting for a fresh breath amongst the stink of diesel and lies. "Just a little dizzy spell." I shivered, even though there was sweat on my forehead and legs. "Is this bridge vibrating?" Mike put an arm round me and we walked to a crash barrier where we rested beneath the shade from the trees. "What was the hospital like?" I pressed.

"Oh, clean, modern, funded by foreign donors no doubt."

"And was it busy?"

"A few people waiting but nothing too major."

"That's lucky."

Mike made me wait while he bought some cans of coke. After wiping the rims with what he told me were the last of his antiseptic wipes he let me drink from mine. "The sugar and caffeine should do you good."

"And you?"

"A little treat. I'll be back on the programme tomorrow. Come on, here's a taxi." We stood by the driver's window while Mike haggled and then got in. But on the way to the hotel he spotted a sign for The Crocodile Farm. "Do you feel up to it? Let you finally see all those animals you've been going on about."

"I could go to a zoo anytime back home," I protested, but Mike was already giving the driver new instructions.

We knew we had arrived when a huge papier-mâché crocodile complete with perfect white triangular teeth came grinning at us as we turned a corner.

"Go quickly and you might catch feeding time at the juvenile's pond," the receptionist told us. So we jogged along to see a zoo keeper emptying buckets containing hundreds of yellow fluffy things, which turned out to be dead chicks, onto the concrete of the pen. The small crocodiles were out of the water in a shot, snapping at the baby birds, tossing them down their throats, their little legs last to go. A toddler in an England top rattled the wire metal fence shouting, "coc-co-dil, coc-co-dil," again and again while his mother fluffed his curls.

We walked to the next pen. The crocodiles here had all eaten and were digesting their food in the sun, mouths agape, so still that they could have been the work of a taxidermist. "Not much to see here," I observed before noticing that one of the crocodiles had six legs. I walked to the railings and saw that a couple of others were albinos, and quite a large number had kinks in their tails. There was even a pair of Siamese twins.

"This is incredible," said Mike. "You see over there?" He pointed to three concrete circular tanks that were set apart from the adventure playground decor of the zoo. They were about the size of sewage filter pools with roofs low over them as if they housed animals that couldn't abide the light. "That's where they keep the normal crocodiles, the ones that get farmed for food. These ones here survive because they are deformed or freaks. It's like the opposite of evolution."

I didn't know anything about that but I was pretty certain there was something wrong about the place. We shambled on to the next enclosure and stood in front of a sign saying *Big Daddy*. The pen had a deep looking pond and lots of undergrowth. Comical warnings were posted on the protective wire fencing saying things like,

No Swimming Today!!!

Please do not feed Big Daddy with your hands!!!

"Can you see anything?" I asked after a couple of minutes.

"No."

"Maybe it's a joke."

Families speculated over whether a floating piece of bark was Big Daddy's head or if a strange shaped rock next to a bush was his foot. The information board told us that Big Daddy was a genuine man-eater, a killer of three Zambians no less. Visitors waited patiently, speaking in hushed voices to show proper deference. Clearly his celebrity status was due to his murderous qualities but I had often seen people crowding around a glass tank in the reptile house containing a stick and a stone or an aquarium in which the only things moving are bubbles. In other cells there are snakes or fish flashing their bright colours. But they are bored of this. They want a glimpse of something that doesn't want to be seen. The thing hidden behind the rock, the colour of dust, the shape so indistinct that we don't know if that's an eye watching us.

"Well Big Daddy, if he's even there, isn't showing face. What's next?"

"Are you hungry?"

I was famished, starving, about to faint on the floor. "I could manage a small bite I suppose."

The zoo had a restaurant which advertised itself with a placard proclaiming,

Juicy Crocodile Burgers and other exotic meats!!!

"I think I'll just have toast and tea," I said.

"But you won't get a chance like this again. I mean it's not like they sell crocodile meat in the Co-op."

We placed our orders and waited. Mike rubbing the plaster which he claimed covered the place where he'd had a blood test. I wondered if, having tricked me into thinking he was fine, he had somehow convinced himself. Certainly he seemed less traumatised than last night.

"Did you have to pay to get the test done?"

"Yeah, but it wasn't too expensive."

"And the needle was sterile?"

"I saw him taking the syringe from the packet."

I shuddered. "I hate blood tests."

"I can't wait to get this burger." He steered the conversation onto another topic. "I was going mad for meat at the Ks'. Really, our red blood count would have been rock bottom if I hadn't brought those iron supplements." I watched his mouth moving, hands waving to illustrate a point, face open and relaxed. A born liar, I thought, a total natural.

At the table next to us two sunburnt men were moving on from competing over who had visited the most obscure countries to bragging about who had eaten the most bizarre meat. In addition to crocodile this restaurant had zebra and ostrich on the menu, but after eulogising about the wonders of grilled ostrich breast versus raw zebra they both moved onto rarer and stranger feasts.

"Barbecued koala," I heard one of them saying, "is certainly far superior to kangaroo, if you ever get stuck in that country."

"If you liked koala you'll love chimpanzee," the other man

assured him.

They both cackled, showing off their stumpy, gold filled teeth. I had no idea if they were joking or not. "I'm going out, catch a breath of air," I said getting up from the air conditioned restaurant and wandering out into the muggy zoo stink of the afternoon.

On my left were a couple of individually caged ostriches. I'd seen films of these beauties running across grasslands at tremendous speeds but here they were stooped like old dowagers. They rustled their dirty feathers as they dipped their beaks to the floor to peck at seeds; the little birds flying between the bars of their cages, stole their food before returning to the sky above. I turned to watch a guide lifting baby crocodiles from a bucket. Female tourists crooned and squealed as one lady had a croc placed on her shoulder. Quick as a flash her husband whipped out a camera and she went from looking quietly appalled to holding the animal in front of her face and planting a kiss, its little legs clawing at the air like a mechanical toy whose batteries are running out.

I wandered on, past the wooden walkways and exotic plants to a field of scrubby grass. In front of me was one of the concrete tanks that Mike had said kept the farmed crocodiles. I heard a Kenyan voice shout, "Miss please, Miss you can't look there!" The walls of the tank were as high as my shoulders. A conical roof was held up over the enclosure by half a dozen metal poles each about two feet in height. I rested my forearms on the top of the wall and hoisted myself up so I could see into the pit. "Miss come away, it is dangerous." The animals were far below me. From up here I could just about make out their black, bloated shapes, and as my eyes became used to the light I saw that there were dozens of them crawling around on top of each other. Two set about thrashing and fighting as if there was something worth winning down there. Another pathetically tried to climb the vertical wall of the pit. An arm wrapped round my waist and pulled me down. I turned expecting to see a Kenyan zoo guide but it was Mike.

He planted me on the ground and stepped back, a look of horror on his face.

"What did you see? What did you see?" He asked. I was aware that the tourists, the ones squealing over the baby crocodiles, were watching.

"No, nothing really. Just vague shapes and darkness, nothing worth mentioning at all."

Chapter Eleven

It was the morning of New Year's Day and I was running through a Kelvin Park crusty with frost, beneath a sky the colour of city pigeons. I wore matching Nike running gloves, hat, leggings, and jacket, all Christmas presents from my dad. I had felt clumsy and inhibited running with all this clothing, and my fingers and face had been cold until I'd been on the go for 15 minutes. First footers froze when they saw me, their faces more amazed than that of the smallest child in the most forgotten village we had run through in Kenya. I jogged past a group of ugly misshapen Goths who inevitably sang "Keep on Running," at me. Only minutes earlier some wee neddette had become the 10 millionth person to shout "Run Forest, run," cackling at her own wit. I decided to do a warm down loop into the city centre. I never normally ran along Sauchiehall Street but figured I'd enjoy slaloming through casualties from the night before, looking at their drink-ravaged faces and saggy bodies.

At Charing Cross a topless man was playing traffic conductor or matador with the snorting traffic. I sprinted to the pedestrian walkway, taking the steps three at a time. A couple of primary school aged girls were leaning over the railings trying to spit on the windscreens of passing cars below. On Renfield Street a man toasted me with what looked like a jam jar filled with whisky before trying to engage me in a fight or a dance, his purpose unclear to either of us. A tall blonde with weird art school clothes was traversing the front of a tenement, her legs juddering, eyes staring in terror at the pavement. For a moment I thought she was Kirsten but her face was more podgy than pixyish.

I hadn't spoken to her since the airport. It was clear we both needed time to breathe after living in each other's pockets for so many weeks. On one level this was a total relief. I actually enjoyed Christmas and was genuinely happy to spend time with my dad. I didn't have to talk much about Kenya. Everyone asked of course, the usual stupid question, "So Kenya, how was it?" to which I would say, "Cool," or "Great," or "You know," and they would nod as if they did.

The boys I ran with plugged me for info about the Kenyan training camps, their methods, diets, racing tactics, anything. I told them as much as I could but they seemed dissatisfied, as if I was keeping something from them. "The great secret is there is no great secret," was the type of thing I would say and they would nod disbelievingly.

After hearing that I wanted a window seat for both flights Kirsten had insisted she would have the same, which, of course, meant we weren't sitting next to each other. Instead I had to endure an English man with halitosis on the flight from Mombasa, who spent most of the journey ranting about how he would spend his next holiday in a civilised country. After flying over the vast darkness of the Sahara, a galaxy of street lights marked out a major Mediterranean city. Following the flight map, I tried to spot major landmarks to help me guess each city as we passed over them. But staring down from that great height, my eyes were drawn to the floodlit running tracks. Every city had one, marking out the same distances with the same pattern of lines laying down their challenge.

On the shuttle up from London, I had to endure death by a thousand nudges as I was sat next to an inconsiderately fat man whose great rolls of blubber hung over my arm rest. But I didn't care by this point, we were almost home. I eventually caught up with Kirsten, who was still buzzing from a conversation I'd tried to eavesdrop on that she'd had with a BBC journalist based in Kenya. We'd had a falling out as we waited competitive as ever to see whose bags would appear first and she elbowed my chivalrous attempts to collect her luggage from the conveyor belt. I watched with arms crossed as she wrestled with a suitcase that weighed half as much as she did. Walking down the Arrivals corridor I glanced at a TV showing who was waiting. Mrs Harrison was there: with her eyebrows plucked into an arc, her hair pulled into a tight blonde bun, her colourful glossy makeup and that permanent wide eyed look, as delightedly amazed with the world as a children's TV presenter. Next to her, but at a subtle distance, my father stood looking like he was doing some complex origami with a tabloid newspaper that he'd probably brought as a prop. They were both delighted to see us.

"Oh but you're thin, isn't she thin Mike? What have they done to you?" Mrs Harrison said, hugging a stiff armed Kirsten. "We'll get you home, feed you up," she promised. "Here let me take that, no I insist." She bundled Kirsten away from us like a minder protecting a celebrity from the paparazzi.

My dad slapped me on the shoulder. "Good journey?"

"Fine," I said, wanting to shout something after Kirsten. She hadn't even said goodbye. It would have been different if Mr Harrison had been there. He would have insisted we got some coffee, talked over the adventure as a group; our feelings about what we had experienced would have been set. His enthusiasm would have infected us, and in telling the stories we would have started to forget the smell of open sewers, the sight of glue addicted street kids. We had often said, when things were bad or sad or confusing, that we would take a long time to sort out the experience in our heads, but talking to Mr Harrison would have helped. All he'd have needed was a story about some runners or some funny experience with an animal or some local customs that we didn't understand and that would be our 3 months in Kenya neatly packaged, an easily deliverable anecdote, enough to fend off any curious friend. As Kirsten and her mother disappeared through large revolving doors I felt a blast of bleak Scottish air, a smell of damp and breweries, and had a strange premonition that I would never see her again.

I turned down Rose Street and jogged comfortably on to an apocalyptically deserted Sauchiehall Street to begin my journey west. The pavement was polka dotted with patches of Pakora puke; pigeons pecked amongst the brightly coloured vomit, celebrating New Year in style; litter bins overflowed with empty cans and bottles.

"This place is finished!" a reveller spinning round a lamp post throwing bank cards and ID at passing taxis shouted. "The world," he yelled gleefully, "it's the end of the fucking world!"

I bounded down the rest of the road, ignoring him. Glasgow prophets slurring Armageddon were nothing new. Two female runners, joggers really, jiggled towards me. I wiped the sweat from my face and picked up my stride. They looked at me and I nodded, a shared respect, a small acknowledgement that we were better than all this.

I kept relaxed, a good easy form, and tried to catch sight of my reflection in shop windows. As I passed an electrical goods store the flashing of TV screens behind grilled windows grabbed my attention. They were tuned to different channels but one telly had caught my eye. There amongst adverts for dog food, interior design shows and one of those kid's film from the Eighties that gets shown every Christmas was something from another world. A road with pot holes and crumbling pavements, on one side The Gladness Barbers and on the other The Wellness Butchers: the doors shut, corrugated sheeting over the windows. No sign of Malpas and the street boys or the hundreds of layabouts who littered the pavements. The picture wobbled like the camera man was running or nervous or both. Then a man appeared, sprinting wildly down the street. At first I hoped this was footage of some New Year's Race, and marvelled at the coincidence, at how small the world really is. But this wasn't a race, the man's shirt had been half torn from him and his pursuers, dozens of young boys, were carrying pangas, picks, scythes. The fleeing man in his panic tripped and fell. He got up but not quickly enough. The film cut back to a shocked looking news reader the moment before the mob started hacking and slashing him to death. An old down-and-out with a biblical beard and holy, hollow cheeks stood next to me.

"Poor bugger," he said. "Poor, poor bugger."

The screen showed other scenes: rubbish strewn streets, one moment deserted, the next filled with rampant, rampaging youths; patchworks of brown and grey that as helicopter cameras zoomed in became the rusty corrugated sheet roofs of burning slums; a boy dabbing at the sticky blood that dribbled from his split head; the faces wild, triumphant, angry, senseless. I turned and thought I was going to be sick.

"You're mad you are. Trying to run after last night," said some skinny-jeaned boy that I vaguely recognised from Uni. My fingers gripped the grilled metal shutter that protected the window. The TV showed footage of soldiers firing their rifles, of a mob disappearing into the thick smoke of burning truck tyres. "Bloody Africa," the boy said. "We should just fucking nuke the place and be done with it." I looked back at the TV but they had moved onto an item about football. "You ok?"

"Yeah," I said, adjusting my face and continuing my run. My heart rate monitor watch said my pulse had topped 180 bpm which was much higher than it should be. I slowed down but couldn't stop the panic rising in my throat.

At home there was an extra wheelie bin I'd borrowed from a neighbour. To help my legs recover after a hard run I always poured cold water and ice into the bin and submerged myself up to the top of my thighs. Before this morning's run I had filled the bin knowing the outside temperature was so low that the water would freeze over. I broke the thin layer of ice with my fist, climbed the fence next to the bin and plunged in. It was pretty much the last thing I wanted to do after running for an hour in sub zero temperatures, but the cold invoked a blood rush that flushed damage-inflicting waste from my system and gave my muscles a controlled constriction, numbing and relieving any soreness. As I was running two or three times a day such radical methods of recovery were necessary.

In any case, I could see the car of my aunt, who was due to arrive today with my Nan, and I was happy enough to delay meeting them. I clenched my teeth as the cold gripped my bollocks in its frozen fist and made the back of my head feel the way it did when I ate ice cream. Steam came off my sweat soaked top and I removed my damp hat as it too began to chill. I kept replaying the film of the man being chased down the High Street in Eldoret. For some reason I wanted to see the clip again. I couldn't explain why, it had genuinely sickened me, but I wanted to see the look on the man's face as he tried to get up from falling and realised his attackers were upon him. I guess I also wanted to see what happened next. Not the mob hacking his body to bits, I mean what they did after that: had they fed their frenzy or did they march on for more?

I was shivering. In practice I should have stayed in the bin for at least 10 minutes but my whole body had begun to tremble. I climbed out, shaking the cold water from my legs and slapping my hamstrings. My dad answered the door, his face greyer and grimmer than usual.

"Mike, we've just heard some terrible news."

"I know," I said pushing past him to dry my legs on a towel, "I saw it through the window of a TV shop."

"It's been on the news?"

"Of course, how did you find out?"

"Alexis Harrison called me. She thought you would want to know, seeing you were so close and everything."

"What are you talking about?"

"Kirsten."

"Kirsten?"

"She was found dead this morning."

"Where?"

"On a hillside, Ben Earb, I think it was called."

"That's on the Cateran Trail." I responded to the question in his eyes by saying, "We went there to train last summer. Did she fall?"

"No, the police don't think so. It seems she drove to Blairgowrie last night and started running."

I remembered the weather report from the night before, the forecaster warning that temperatures could drop to minus 9 degrees on the mountains of Scotland and that there would be snow, and my dad sneeringly saying, 'Aye and there'll be a lot of people spending Hogmanay on a hill."

"That's impossible," I heard myself saying. "Kirsten's not stupid. She'd never run there at night time, it'd be too dark, too isolated."

"Her mum said she left the house at nine last night, told them she was meeting friends in a pub. She was found a few hours ago by a group of hikers." And here he lowered his voice so my Nan and aunt couldn't hear. "She was only wearing a pair of running shorts and a vest. The clothes and shoes that she had left the house in were left in her car. No sign of anyone else involved or anything malicious." He said the last bit like a news reporter, his eyes gaping at mine to see if I had understood.

"But Ben Earb, that's about twenty miles from where they found her car." I started to protest, but the image of her stepping bare-footed out of the warmth of her car and onto a snowy path, stopped me in my tracks.

"Twenty miles?"

"Over hilly, broken ground."

The Cateran Trail was an ancient 65 mile path that had been used by bands of Highland cattle thieves. I had run it with Kirsten and a couple of other boys last summer; it had taken us four days. The route took you through rough moorland, secluded glens and over high mountain passes.

I closed my eyes and imagined her running those desolate paths, slipping, tripping in the dark, but getting up and continuing, because that is what you did. Her feet so numb that she wouldn't notice them bleeding as she padded over the snow smothered landscape, the silence punctured only by the pop of distant fireworks as the rest of the country celebrated

Hogmanay. I thought of her running the steady slope of Ben Earb, exhausted, staggering before finally lying in some snowy hollow, shivering, teeth chattering, limbs going numb as she waited.

"But she was half a lassie when she came back from Kenya, poor lamb. Just a wee slip of a thing. How would she have made it so far?"

I wandered off to my room, locking the door on my relatives' shouts that I come down and talk to them. Scanning my shelves, I found a Manual of Nursing Practices I'd taken out of the library. I flicked to the chapter I was looking for, but there was too little information and too many variables. Nothing about body weight, and I didn't know if she was wet or if it was windy. I wondered, why that Trail? It was very picturesque, isolated, surrounded by gloomy, looming hills. I re-read the Manual. There were a couple of case histories, one from a man who had survived profound hypothermia and reported that after the initial pain he had experienced a deep numbness, a childish appreciation of everything and an uncontrollable need to giggle. I returned the book to its shelf. I guess I could never know – had never known – how she felt.

My aunt shouted, "Kettle's boiled!"

I put on a dry tracksuit and trudged obediently down the stairs.

"Some sugary tea, that's what you need." She shovelled heaped teaspoonfuls into my mug as if that would help. She took the tea bags out and pegged them on a line to be used again. I went into the sitting room, and leant down to let my Nan peck me on the cheek, her lips somehow reminding me of the teabags that hung in the kitchen curling in on themselves, like bats sleeping. We sat in the suffocating heat of the room as some game show blazed in the background. My aunt and Nana smelt of talcum powder and ripe peaches. Normally, they nattered away, exchanging scandals and deaths with all the indifference of people playing a card game. But today they were silent but for the slurping of tea, the shifting of pillows and my father solicitously asking if everyone was comfortable and should we not perhaps make one final assault on the Christmas cake.

"Put the fairy lights on if you've got nothing better to do. It's awful gloomy without the fairy lights," my Nan chided him. The two old women were clearly uncomfortable. Death was usually their territory but a young person's death couldn't be capped with the usual stoicisms. The game show stopped, and the news came on. I wondered if there'd be any explanation for the violent scene I'd witnessed on the Electrical Shop's telly. I knew the election they'd all been so obsessed with had taken place four days earlier, but I hadn't seen any reports of trouble until today. Chaos in Kenya was the lead item. I guess the colonial links, the fact that many Brits still lived there and even more went on holiday there made the story newsworthy.

The newsreader, a handsome, serious looking lady read from her autocue that the results of the election were being widely disputed and that Odaiga, the candidate who practically everyone we'd met supported, had lost the election and was crying foul. As many as 300 people were already dead and 75,000 had fled their homes. Violence, the newsreader said, had broken out along tribal lines, with neighbour attacking neighbour. The Kalenjins, the fabled running tribe, seemed to be responsible for some of the worst atrocities.

With a warning that we may find some of these images disturbing, they flashed to the same scene of the man running down that road I'd cycled on so many times; his last moments on earth to be relayed and repeated in living rooms across the globe.

"Do we have to watch this?" my aunt complained. "There's Celebrity Strictly on the other side."

"Eldoret," my dad said, waving his hand at her to shut up. "Was that not where you were?"

"Not exactly," I mumbled.

"And X Factor might be on as well."

A reporter with a wizened face and troubled eyes, who seemed to spend her life being whisked from one disaster zone to another, stalking death like a hyena, licked her lips and told the world about the smouldering building behind her. It took me a few seconds to recognise the smoky remains as the corrugated iron barn we cycled past on the road into Eldoret, the one that Mrs K and the best dressed orphans worshipped in every Sunday.

"They'd fled to the church for refuge. The remains of blackened cooking pots and singed clothes, showing where 200 Kikuyus, the prime minister's tribe, had sought to escape the violence of the streets. But for 35 people escape was possible. A mob of Kalenjin youths surrounded the church blocking windows and exits with paraffin soaked mattresses. One woman told me how she escaped, only to have her baby snatched from her and thrown into the flaming building. This is where she perished." The camera scanned over Red Cross workers sifting through the remains: a child's shoe, half a dozen bikes chained to stop people stealing them now charred black.

"Bloody animals," my Nan said.

"Savages," my aunt agreed. "The devil is here on earth and doing his work amongst us."

"I need a shower." I slipped out of the room.

A hot shower 20 – 30 minutes after the ice bath completes the process and further helps the muscles recover. I was only just starting to take hot water for granted. Soon I would forget urging my sweating body into the freezing shower at the Ks'. The water pattered on my head. Kenya was in chaos and Kirsten was dead and I felt – what, lonely? That didn't make sense. Maybe I was in shock, maybe that could explain why I felt so detached.

I thought a lot about the funeral. I'd never been to one for anyone aged under sixty. Kirsten's mum would want to speak to me, probably Mr Harrison as well. Would there be an inquest? I didn't know how these things worked. I'd spent the most time with her over the last 3 months but I hadn't seen her for 12 days. Maybe something terrible had happened in that time, something that I knew nothing about. Could I have said that I'd known her best? It seemed unlikely, but if not me, who else? I kept replaying the dozens of painful conversations we'd had. Was there something I could have said? Was there something that signposted where she was going? With the vantage of hindsight it seemed there was a fucking map.

As I towelled myself dry I heard my aunt say, "It's a shame for the lad, a shame and a shock. That's why suicide is a sin because it's those that are left behind that suffer. It's them that have to put the pieces together."

My Nan murmured an agreement and my dad irrelevantly said, "Nothing's confirmed Jean, we can't be certain it's that, not yet."

"But can you imagine what's going on in a lassie's head to do something like that?" My aunt ploughed on. "I mean, a bright University lassie, always winning races – and not just in Scotland. A nice successful family, famous dad, famous grandad, good people." She tutted. "It just goes to show," she said, although what it went to show she didn't seem to know. But my Nan realised they had a mystery here, something they could spend the rest of their afternoon sinking their dentures into.

"Nobody knows what goes on behind closed doors," she enigmatically said.

Over the next few days came more news reports, more mob slayings, lines of women and children carrying their possessions on their backs, gangs of men waving their weapons in the air. Rioters screamed at cameras, their words incomprehensible in their froth of rage. A woman the same age as Mrs K said that her people accepted death. She spoke firmly about how they were prepared to march against the discredited election and the army with their tear gas and bullets. As pictures from Eldoret came in I strained to see familiar faces amongst the crowds but there was no one I knew. A famous marathoner, Wesley Kimutai, was killed by a poisoned arrow; others spoke of the impossibility of training, the fear of attack. Rwanda was what people were most afraid of: a repeat of genocide on that scale. The world's media descended en masse.

Friends who knew I had been there said they were shocked and disgusted by the violence. But like me when I was in the country, they couldn't remember the names of the politicians or the competing tribes, or even see why all these tribes were lumped together into one country any way. So they fell back on disgust, at the savagery of uneducated Africans, animals, beasts, primeval they called them. The problems of that continent were so great that a few called for its obliteration, but what they really wanted was for it to be obliterated from their conscience. 24 Hour Rolling News showed us the worst of it, the type of slaughter that we read about and saw in grainy photos of pogroms, fire bombings, genetic cleansing in our own continent but that seemed like something consigned to the past, acts that another species had committed. That was one reason why the footage provoked such outrage and disgust - The reminder that in times of terror we all have the potential to behave like that.

But this wasn't a feeling people liked and so we switched over and besides, if you've seen one man getting hacked to bits by a mob you've seen them all. Along the bottom of our screens flashed sports bulletins – Sharapova wins in Hong Kong – United boosted by Tevez injury report. The violence went on for weeks but our attention waned as newer and more sensational stories appeared to feed our information addictions.

Kirsten had the email addresses of most of the people we had met, at least the ones who had email addresses. She had written them down in the journal in which she recorded Kiswahili phrases, the names of places and people and moments that she didn't want to forget. At the cremation I had asked Mr Harrison if I could borrow the book. He had looked at me reproachfully but replied *yes*.

Hundreds of people attended the funeral, most of them her parents' age or older. The girls who had trained with her and dropped out and a couple of old school friends who had drifted made up the younger crowd. A lot of people were crying and the priest was talking about what a gift she had been, how lucky we were to have her in our lives.

Erin Maclavety, the girl we'd talked about on that last night in Mombasa, hugged me against her heaving chest and said, "You must really miss her, now that she's gone."

I really missed her before she was gone, we all did, was a thought that came later, but at the time I just nodded.

Mr Harrison was at the Crematorium door, pumping hands, his jaw working nervously. He shook my hand and said, "Good of you to come," as if he didn't recognise me. A few weeks later, when I called to collect the journal, he told me that he wouldn't be coming back to coaching, he hoped that I understood.

I do, I said. *We split by mutual consent.*

He paused. *By mutual consent? Yes, I suppose we do.*

He handed me the journal, not looking at me, not looking at the book.

Holding the journal, which I had seen so often in her hands, felt like a terrifying privilege. As I flicked through those pages, scanning the scrawled writing that she had always shielded me from, I suddenly realised she was dead. I focussed on finding the email addresses, but the pages on which they must have been recorded had been ripped out. I couldn't understand why Kirsten would have done this and wondered what else those pages had contained. What was left were descriptions of the days we had spent, appeals to some unspecified reader for understanding, accounts of what appeared to be nightmares. I slammed the book shut and resolved to read no more. I had promised to return it to the Harrisons but instead hid it on my bookshelf.

I did have one email address. It was Gladys K's. She had given it to me at the embarrassing dance party when I had promised to send the photos. It was a new address: Moses had set it up on a computer at the farm on one of the few occasions that the internet was working. He had said that his old mother was now in the 21st century and she had looked at him sceptically unsure if this was a good thing or not.

I uploaded photos from my camera to our PC: the gang that had stopped us at the road block, the prize winning ceremony in Iten, the staged running photos, Kirsten unaware that a picture was being taken, deep in thought and beautiful. I looked through them all. My Nan and Aunt leaned over my shoulder, won over by the children's beautiful smiles, their pretty hand-me-down clothes, their obvious joy when they danced. "Like little angels," my Aunt said.

"Innocent as angels," my Nan confirmed. "It's enough to break your heart."

But I didn't send these photos. At the time I told myself that Gladys K would never check her inbox, that the telephone wires would be down as they always were and that the internet cafe in Eldoret was too dangerous to visit. But these were poor excuses. People often talk about the poignancy of photographs, the subjects frozen at one moment with all kinds of fates awaiting them. Neither we nor the people in the photos can guess what horrors or glories lurk round the corner. A picture may well be worth a thousand words but only if you like the sound of your own voice speculating, inventing, creating endings.

It's different looking at photos of yourself as a child or the face of a friend who has killed herself. In these there is no room for invention, only the poignancy of what could have been. Years later when their brothers and sisters had died of Aids and they were sitting about the streets their teeth the colour of Coca-Cola, would they want photos of when they were young and beautiful and smiled with abandon as if there was nothing to fear?

So, I saved the photos on a memory stick and once the storage space was full lost it at the bottom of a drawer and for a very long time tried not to remember any of these faces ever again.

ABOUT THE AUTHOR

Ewan Gault is an award winning Scottish writer. He was born in Kuwait and over the last decade has lived in Japan, Italy, Kenya, Ethiopia, The Western Highlands and now Oxford. Writing is the only way he can get back to all the places he has been.

Since graduating with a distinction from Glasgow University's Creative Writing Masters in 2006, his short stories have been widely published and performed. 'Distance,' his debut novel, follows two British athletes training in a Kenyan running camp. Trying to make their way home while the country around them plunges towards a violently disputed election, the novel's narrators find themselves drifting further apart when they need each other most. 'Distance' was inspired by the time Ewan spent training at a high altitude centre in Kenya's Rift Valley, an area that is home to the legendary Kalenjin "running tribe," who, since 1980, have won 40% of distance running men's medals at World and Olympic Championships.

Lightning Source UK Ltd.
Milton Keynes UK
UKOW04f1324091213

222648UK00002B/13/P